Dear Reader,

Although *Rooms of the Heart* was first published in 1990, the love of Tempest and Braxton is still as fresh and enduring as it was then. I truly hope you enjoy entering their world. To me, *Rooms* was the equivalent of having your very first child and will always be the book of which I am most proud. It set the pace for me and allowed the industry to take notice of the beauty of the African-American Romance.

Thank you again for your continued support. Please be on the lookout for *Indiscretions* coming this fall, also being released for the second time.

Until next time,

Donna

Dedication

With much affection to the countless fans who have stuck with me all these years. It was that constant support which has made the reissuing of *Rooms of the Heart* possible. And thank you to Genesis Press for having the foresight to bring it back.

Many thanks,

Donna

Chapter One

The silken fingers of first light peeked through the partially drawn blinds, stretching their way across the spacious bedroom to caress Tempest out of her solitary slumber. Raven hair billowed out around her oval face in a shadowed halo, as she burrowed her way further under the floral quilt, trying desperately to hold on to the fleeting remnants of sleep. For as long as she slept, she could keep Braxton close to her—the scent and warmth of him invading her pores, unlocking the hidden corridors of her soul.

She reached for him in that magical world between the conscious and the unconscious, but found only empty space. In that brief instant of clarity, she came fully awake. She had only dreamed of him again. A dream so powerful it left her trembling in its aftermath, leaving her with a hopelessness that should have long ago been buried. But Braxton was, and always would be, a part of her. This was a fact that she'd come to live with every day of her life.

Unable to hold back the realities of another day any longer, Tempest pulled herself up with a sigh, stretched her long limbs, and sat on the edge of her canopied bed, willing her dreams back into her subconscious. Still the visions of Braxton persisted, etched on her brain as clearly as if she'd just seen him, instead of six long years ago.

Cupping her face in her palms, she wondered once again if the longing would ever end. Her marriage to David had suffered as a result of it, and he deserved better than that. He'd been more than understanding, always willing to do whatever was in his power to make her happy. A power that seemed boundless—the thought of which brought her fully into the present.

Pulling a terry robe around her slender figure, she quietly made her way to the kitchen, mindful of the still sleeping household. Somehow, she vowed, as she tiptoed past her daughter's bedroom door, she would find a way to tell David before it was too late for both of them.

When she entered the kitchen, she was surprised to find her housekeeper, Mrs. Harding, already busy with breakfast.

Without looking up she said, "You never could sleep late after one of those trips of yours. I figured you'd be up and about, so I started breakfast." Turning to point a pudgy finger at Tempest, Clara Harding added, "Now don't you touch a thing until I finish." She turned her ample frame back to face the stove.

"And good morning to you too," Tempest said, while swiping a piece of toast from the platter and plopping down onto the kitchen stool. "You never cease to amaze me, Clara. But you're right, my body clock still hasn't adjusted. If I were back in South America," she said between bites, "I'd be halfway through my morning."

Without a backward glance, Clara asked, "That toast is just the way you like it, isn't it? There's some jam in the cupboard."

"How do you do that?" Tempest giggled between mouthfuls. "It's like ESP or something."

"Girl, I've known you since you were no bigger than that little vixen of yours. A body would think you'd have learned your lessons by now. Humph."

"Some people just never learn, do they?" Tempest said with mock sarcasm.

"Don't get sassy with me."

"Speaking of sassy, how is she?" Tempest's eyes glowed at the thought of her daughter. "My flight was so late last night, I didn't have the heart to wake her when I got in."

"Kai is as mischievous as ever," Clara said, whipping the eggs in the pan. "Askin' about you every time I turn around. This has been a long month."

"I know. I didn't want to go, but I had to—you

3

know that. That design job was very important to my company. She wasn't too upset, was she?"

"As upset as a five-year-old can get, I suppose. For the most part, she was up to some trick or the other. She didn't give herself enough time to be lonely for you."

"That's comforting," Tempest added dryly. "But I still can't wait to see her."

Tempest rose from her stool and went to the cabinets in search of the jam.

"She'll be up as soon as she gets a whiff of this bacon." With one hand, Clara spooned out the eggs onto the platter. With the other hand, she meticulously lined up the bacon in the frying pan, as straight as soldiers.

"Is David home?" Tempest asked hesitantly, while spreading the thick apple jam on her second slice of toast.

"Not that I know of. He came in last night and went out again." Then she added with a shake of her head, "I've never seen two people who have so much in common, not able to iron out their problems."

"Sometimes it's not that simple, Clara. I wish that it were," she said softly.

"He's a good man. You couldn't ask for a better husband. It would be a shame to lose him." Clara turned to face Tempest, beefy hands on her broad hips. "You think I don't know what's bothering you? I remember when you came back from school. You weren't the same person, and you haven't been the same since. Six

4

years is a long time to carry a torch for a man who doesn't give a damn about you, honey. Don't ruin your marriage because of that.

"There. I've said my piece. It's none of my business anyway," she said, finally satisfied that she'd gotten that off of her chest.

Tempest was the daughter she never had, and she loved her like her own. She would do anything for her and Kai, even if it meant butting into Tempest's business every now and then.

Tempest hung her head. Clara knew her better than she knew herself. She'd never been able to hide anything from her all-seeing eyes. She'd been one of the few people who had suspected what had happened to her. But not even Clara knew the whole story. She'd been too devastated to tell anyone at first—not even her best friend, Bridgette. In her heart she knew that Clara was right. Braxton wasn't coming back. He'd never made any effort to contact her in all these years. It was David who had been there for her: marrying her, getting her business off the ground, loving her unquestionably. Nonetheless, it was Braxton who had stolen her heart on the grassy hills of Virginia. It was Braxton whom she still loved. But she owed David, if not her love, at least her loyalty. They had to find a way to work things out between them.

She was due in his office at 11:00 a.m. for their meeting with the new architect that David had found while she was away. She'd talk to David today, she decided.

Finally, looking up, Tempest said, "You're right as usual. But it's been difficult for me, too. I know a lot of our problems have been my fault. I'll find a way to work it out—somehow. I plan to talk to him today."

"The sooner the better. Things are getting pretty strained around here. One more thing before I shut my mouth. As much as I care about David, you've always had a special place in my heart, you know that. You have to do what's best for you, never mind what anyone else thinks. Don't forget that. Don't stay with a man that you don't love, but don't pine over someone who doesn't love you either. Now put a smile on that pretty face of yours. Everything will be fine. I have faith in you."

"Thanks for your vote of confidence," Tempest said with the beginning of a smile. "Now mercifully changing the topic from my marital woes, did David mention to you who the architect was that he found? The connection was so poor when he called me, it was a miracle that I understood that we were to meet today."

"You know he never discusses business with me. Knowing David, I'm sure he found the perfect person."

"I never doubted that for a minute," Tempest said wryly.

Then just as Clara had predicted, in unison with the sizzling aroma of bacon, running footsteps could be heard pounding down the hallway. Tempest's heart raced in anticipation.

"What did I tell you? Here comes the little tornado now. Brace yourself," Clara warned with a chuckle, placing the breakfast fixings on the table.

"Miss Clara! Miss Clara! I'm up!" came the squeaky five-year-old voice. Just then Kai burst through the kitchen door and came to a grinding halt. Her dark eyes widened in surprise, while her mouth broke into a wide grin, exhibiting a missing front tooth.

"M-o-m-m-y!" she squealed, hurtling herself across the short distance, straight into her mother's outstretched arms.

Tempest smothered her in all the hugs and kisses that she'd been saving since the day she'd left, crushing the little body against her own. She inhaled the scent of innocence, as her body shook with the intensity of the love she felt for her daughter.

"Mommy, you're squeezing me again," Kai wailed.

"I'm sorry, baby." She gave her one last hug. "I'm just so happy to see you."

Kai looked up into her mother's eyes. "You don't have to cry just because I lost a tooth," Kai admonished with all the wisdom of her five years. "It didn't even hurt. Right, Miss Clara?" She looked to Clara for confirmation.

"That's not the way I heard it. All that screaming and yelling. Whew!" Clara said, stifling a chuckle.

"It was only one tear," Kai whispered to her mother, holding up one tiny finger in her defense. "Just

7

one."

Tempest looked into her daughter's ebony eyes, seeing her one link to a happier time in their inky depths, and loved her all the more. How many times had she questioned her decision? Now it was too late. Too many years had passed. She'd made the right decision. Hadn't she? A decision that had changed the lives of so many people, and she had more to make in the months ahead.

"Mommy! You're not listening," Kai cried, snapping Tempest out of her reverie.

"I'm sorry, baby. I was just thinking about how big and beautiful you are." She gave Kai a squeeze. "Forgive me?" She smiled down at her daughter.

"Okay," Kai conceded with a nod of her dark head.

"Now hop up on my lap and tell me what you were saying."

"I saw Daddy on television last night."

"You did? Was it exciting?"

"Yeah. I'm gonna tell my friends in school. But there's one thing I don't understand. The voice on the television said that Daddy was running and to vote for him. What's Daddy running from?"

Tempest threw back her head in laughter. "Daddy's not running from anything. He's running for Congress. Remember I told you that Daddy wanted to help people and that he thought he would be able to do that if he won the election? That's why everyone has to decide if they want him in Congress. That's what they will do when they vote."

"Everybody likes my daddy because he builds pretty buildings. So he has to win. Doesn't he, Mommy?"

"We hope so, sweetheart." Tempest wasn't sure if she meant that sentiment or not.

Then just like a five-year-old, Kai's mind flitted to another subject.

"I'm hungry," Kai declared. Clara and Tempest burst out in laughter.

Many hugs, kisses and fits, of laughter later, Kai was hustled off to the school bus by her very reluctant mother. Tempest waved frantically at the departing bus and threw countless kisses, long after the bus was out of sight. On her way back upstairs to their loft apartment, she smiled to herself when she realized how she felt as the bus pulled away, knowing deep inside that Kai had completely put her mother out of her little head as soon as she saw her school friends.

Just as she was about to leave for her office, Clara stopped her in the foyer, her heavy arms laden with laundry.

"Well, you're off bright and early. I thought your meeting was at eleven."

"It is, but I have to stop by my office first to pick up some sketches. I tried to reach David at his office. He isn't in yet." Tempest could not meet the questioning look in Clara's eyes. She reached for her briefcase and jacket to hide her discomfort. "If he should call before I contact him, would you tell him to send a car to my office to pick me up about ten-thirty?"

"If he calls, I'll be sure to tell him."

A silent understanding hung between them. Tempest looked into Clara's loving eyes.

"Thanks."

Clara watched the receding back as Tempest stepped across the threshold. Her heart ached for her, as she shook her head in sadness. As she slowly closed the door, she wondered how such a loving woman who had the world at her feet could be so unhappy.

$$\times\!\!\sim\!\!\!\times$$

The quick cab ride to downtown Manhattan put Tempest in her office long before her staff. These were the moments she loved best, she thought, as she glided through the hushed corridor to the office that bore her name. Those peaceful hours before the city reared its head and burst with life always held a special fascination for her.

As she neared her office, that old familiar rush of exhilaration overcame her. No matter how many times Tempest sat in her presidential chair, or saw her name emblazoned on the door of Dailey Design, Inc., the sensation of pride never left her. Who would have thought that the little girl from Flatbush would wind up on the fortieth floor of the World Trade Center, running one of the most sought-after design firms in New York?

She stepped into her plush office and took in her surroundings. The lush carpet tickled her ankles as she kicked off her shoes and sank into its depths. Leisurely she strolled toward her built-in stereo system, and with one touch of a hidden button behind the oak paneled doors, the room was bathed in a soft, sensuous flow of music.

The touch of another button drew back the silk, floor-to-ceiling drapes, washing the soft pastel room in the early spring sunshine.

Tempest then began her morning ritual of watering the countless plants which gave the enormous room a sense of the tropics amid the chaos of the throbbing city.

Her lithe body moved in graceful rhythm to the mellow tones, as she made her way to the low, sleek couch. Stretching out on its cottony comfort, she briefly recalled the lean years.

It hadn't been easy trying to convince people that she was serious back then. A young girl with high hopes, a lot of talent, but no name, was not a readily accepted commodity. But it was David who had discovered her at an exhibit sponsored by FIT, the design school she had attended. Ironically it was also David who had unwittingly led her to Braxton when he insisted that she return to school to fine-tune her talents as a designer.

Life was so strange, she thought, and often cruel

at the games it played with people's lives. But as she was finally beginning to discover, you had to rule your life, not let it rule you.

Just then the shrill ring of the phone pulled her from her sobering thoughts. She crossed the room to her desk and picked up the phone. The cool, crisp voice of her husband greeted her.

"I called the house. Clara gave me your message."

"I thought I would see you last night when I got in," she said softly.

"I thought it best that I shouldn't be there." He cleared his throat. "The car will be there for you. I'll see you when you get here. Good-bye, Tempest."

"David, wait." Silence.

"Yes?"

Her heart pounded in her chest. This was the first step. She couldn't back out now.

"David, we need to talk. I did a lot of thinking while I was away. We can't go on living like this. Please come home tonight." Silence. "Or maybe we could meet somewhere?"

David's throat tightened. *Maybe. Just maybe,* he thought.

"I have to go out of town tonight on business. I'll make dinner reservations at Jezebel's for eight tomorrow night." He tried to sound noncommittal. "We'll see what happens then." Jezebel's was her favorite place. If he was going to win this fight, he would use everything at his disposal.

"That sounds perfect."

"And, Tempest..."

Her heart lifted. "Yes?"

"Don't keep the driver waiting. This meeting is very important. He'll pick you up *promptly* at ten-thirty."

"I wouldn't dream of it, David." It took all she had not to slam the phone in his ear. Why did it always have to be this way between them? She wanted to scream.

"See you in an hour." He hung up the phone.

Tempest sat in her high-back leather chair, trying to control her rising temper. Maybe this whole idea of a reconciliation was pointless, she thought miserably. It had gotten to a point where she and David were never on the same wavelength. It had been so long since they had really communicated that they didn't know what to say to each other anymore.

She spun the chair to face the window. If she left him now, his chances of winning the election were nil. If she stayed, and he won, she would be tied to him indefinitely. *Is that what I really want?* She had been so sure earlier. Now she didn't know. She massaged her temples.

Finally she decided she had to try. He deserved that much. He'd stood by her when she needed someone. Now it was her turn.

✕

Sounds of activity in the outer office caught her attention. The staff had begun to arrive. Tempest checked her watch. She still had enough time to check her sketches before it was time for her to leave.

After a few moments at her drafting table, Marsha, her secretary, peeked into her office.

"Ms. Dailey, it's so good to see you! I didn't expect you in this morning." A welcoming smile lit up her otherwise plain face, as she rushed over to wrap Tempest in a bony hug.

Tempest returned the embrace, her spirits lifting at the warm reception. One thing that she truly prided herself on was the rapport that she maintained with her staff. Her company was a team, a family, and everyone was a member. It was times like this that made it all worthwhile.

"It's good to see you, too," Tempest said, taking a step back and catching Marsha's hand in her own. "Come and sit for a minute. Catch me up on the gossip."

Three cups of coffee later, Tempest's ears were ringing with office news—from Marsha's surprise engagement, to the scandal in the office down the hall between a mail clerk and the VP's secretary.

"I take it that a lot has been going on since I've been gone. Congratulations again, Marsha. It couldn't have happened to a nicer person. I wish you all the best."

"Oh, thank you, Ms. Dailey. We're both very happy."

Tempest rose from her seat. "I really hate to cut this chat short, but I've got to meet my husband in a half-hour. The car will be here any minute."

"I didn't mean to keep you. It was just so good talking with you."

Tempest smiled.

"This is the meeting about the new housing complex, isn't it?"

"This is it," Tempest said, picking up her portfolio and sketches.

"It will be great if David, I mean, Mr. Lang, is able to get this project off the ground. It would mean so much to a lot of people. He's a great man. You're really lucky. Just imagine if he becomes a congressman. Wouldn't that be wonderful?"

"Yes, I suppose it would," Tempest said absently. "Well, I've got to run. Tell Bridgette that I should be back in the office about two. We'll go over the plans for the island estate then." Tempest grabbed her jacket and headed for the door. "Where is Bridgette, by the way?"

"She had an appointment this morning—potential new client," Marsha called to the quickly departing figure.

"Just what we need," Tempest said over her shoulder. "More work!" She gave Marsha an encouraging smile and darted into the open elevator.

Marsha watched her leave. *What a great lady. I wouldn't trade her in for anyone,* she thought.

✺

As promised, the car and driver were waiting. Within minutes the limousine glided to a halt in front of David Lang's Madison Avenue office building.

On the ride up to his penthouse suite of offices, Tempest ran a quick mental check of the points she wanted to discuss. She and Bridgette had worked too hard in the past few months to leave anything to chance. David was notorious for his ability to talk the unsuspecting right out of their shoes. That knack alone was a necessity in politics. In that instance, he would be perfect. However, she was determined to hold her ground and get her proposals on the table.

The doors of the elevator opened soundlessly as Tempest alighted on the penthouse floor. She took a deep, cleansing breath and strode purposefully forward, her long-legged stride muffled by the thick oriental carpet.

As she approached the glass-enclosed reception area, Annie, the newest in an array of secretaries, rose to greet her.

"Mrs. Lang, I mean, Ms. Dailey." Her cheeks aflame, the young girl covered her face in embarrassment. "I did it again, didn't I?"

Tempest only smiled and reached out to touch

Annie's cheek. After six months Annie still couldn't quite decide what to call her. It had been a constant source of embarrassment for both of them. This time Tempest decided to give her a little help.

"It would be a lot easier if you just called me Tempest."

"Really? I mean, I didn't think—"

"Don't worry about it. That's what all my friends call me."

"If you're sure it's okay." Then she whispered, "Mr. Lang would have a fit if he heard me. You know how Mr. Lang is about protocol."

"You let me worry about that. Is he in his office?"

"Yes. And he's in there with the most gorgeous man I've ever seen," she sighed. "If I wasn't already in love—" Annie rolled her blue eyes up in her head in a feigned faint.

"Then I guess I'd better hurry in and see for myself," Tempest grinned.

"Just go on in. They're waiting for you."

"Thanks, Annie."

"Thank you!"

Tempest strolled down the long corridor toward David's office, waving and smiling at familiar faces on the way. As she neared David's office, she heard voices deep in conversation. Drawing closer to the open door, a paralyzing numbness stopped her in her tracks. The voice...too familiar. She stepped closer and the figures in the room became clearer. A cold sweat broke out on her forehead.

His back was turned, his head held at that all too familiar angle as though listening to something no one else could hear. Tempest felt the floor sway beneath her. Her pulse pounded in her ears, and black spots danced before her eyes. *It couldn't be,* she wanted to scream. She didn't know how long she stood there watching her past and present merge into one, until she heard David's voice pierce the fog that had descended on her.

"Tempest. You're here. Well, don't just stand there, come in. I want you to meet our new partner."

She saw him rise as if in slow motion and turn toward her. Her heart beat in triple time with his every movement. *Don't let this be happening,* she prayed. *Not now. Please not now. Let me be wrong.*

He turned to face her, and a tidal wave of emotion crashed against her. In that brief instant that their eyes met, the world stood still—and she was back in Virginia, loving and being loved by the man her heart would not let go.

"Tempest, I'd like you to meet Braxton Thorne. Braxton, my wife."

Chapter Two

He'd lived this moment a thousand times in his mind. He'd seen her, felt her, inhaled her scent in his dreams and every waking hour. Yet nothing could have prepared him for the kaleidoscopic emotion that welled up inside of him at the nearness of her. She was more beautiful than he remembered. The pale yellow knit dress clung to her shapely figure, emphasizing the svelte contours of her form. His body ached with the longing that he had held in abeyance for far too long. Their eyes sought each other's and locked in a bond that could only be found between two people who have shared their very being between them. In that brief moment of eye contact, they soared in unison through time and space to a place where love was simple and life was full of unending promise.

It had started as a clear day. The University of

Virginia campus was bustling with weekend activity. Students rushed, walked, and ran to friends, lovers, and empty apartments all in search of a diversion for the two-day break ahead.

Braxton, just finished with his last architectural class, was exiting the building just as the first raindrops began to fall. He stood momentarily under the shelter of the leaves, undecided whether he should wait out the rain or meet his friend, Scott Hamilton, when out of the corner of his eye he caught a flash of red. It was her—that girl again.

Red was her favorite color, and Tempest made a point of wearing it often. It brought out her black hair and highlighted her coppery complexion. Tempest floated on air, oblivious to the drizzle or the pointed stare that followed her, as she recalled the words of praise that she'd just received from her design instructor. He'd said her work was magnificent, her eye for detail remarkable. He'd assured her that she would go a long way in the design business if she kept up the good work. His words had made her day. Professor Markam was reputed to be one of the most difficult instructors on campus.

Walking with a light step, her oversized portfolio tucked securely under her arm, she made her way toward her tiny studio apartment several blocks away. As she crossed the grass-covered campus, a strong gust of wind whipped through her unbound hair, tossing it wildly about her face.

Braxton stood entranced, rooted to the spot as he watched her fluid movements. He wanted to call out to her but found himself uncharacteristically speechless. For the first time in his life, he didn't know what to do. He grew angry with himself at his own indecisiveness as he watched her move farther from his sight.

Looking up, she saw heavy, gray clouds approaching.

"I'll never make it home. I'll be drenched," she moaned.

The light spring shower quickly turned to a downpour, confirming her suspicions. Changing directions, she hurried toward Ciro's Café, the local campus hangout. She decided to wait out the storm in there.

Braxton, seeing his chance quickly slipping away, finally came to his senses and took off after her, nearly losing sight of her in the pouring rain.

Just as she reached the entrance door, a strong hand gripped her shoulder. She turned with a start and stared up into bottomless obsidian pools, as a flash of lightning illuminated the heavens, giving the stranger an ethereal quality. A slight shudder raced through her, as the creamy rich voice embraced her senses.

"I thought I'd never catch up with you," was the breathless salute.

Her stomach lurched and lodged in her throat, while her heart beat a staccato rhythm in her chest. When she tried to speak, her voice sounded unnatural and stilted to her ears.

"Do I know you?" *Of course you don't know him, silly,* she chided herself. But she was completely at a loss for something sophisticated to say.

"No, you don't. I've been waiting for an opportunity to meet you. But you're always dashing off somewhere," he finished in a hurried voice. Then with more self-assurance, he said, "I'm Braxton Thorne, and *you're* Tempest Dailey."

Suspicion rose to her throat and registered in the high pitch of her normally husky voice. She clutched her portfolio tightly against her chest.

"How do you know my name?"

"Don't worry. I'm not a mad rapist or anything," he quipped, hypnotizing her with a grin, as a dimple winked at her from under his right eye. "Whether you know it or not, your name has become synonymous with interior design around here."

She felt the heat rise to her face at the unabashed compliment from the handsome man. Her sharp eye took him in all at once. He was tall, at least six-three she noted with pleasure, and as dark as a starless night. He had flawless silky skin, and his broad mouth was etched with a well-trimmed mustache, the full bottom lip promising unseen pleasure. Then somewhat regaining her usual confidence, she toyed with him. A hint of mischief lit her hazel eyes. "Is that the reason you followed me, because of my talents?"

"That's part of it," he said, looking somewhat shaken by the bold look in her eyes. "But—"

He was cut off by two annoyed students who stood waiting at the entrance, dripping from the deluge.

"It seems that we're blocking traffic." He stepped aside to let the couple pass. "Why don't we go inside. It's really coming down. That's if you don't mind. I'd really like to talk with you."

Tempest hesitated but a moment. Something special was happening, like watching the breaking of a new dawn. It frightened yet thrilled her, and she wasn't ready to let it go—not just yet.

"Sure. Why not? You seem safe enough." Over greasy cheeseburgers and crispy french fries, Braxton tried to explain his behavior, stumbling and hesitating along the way, completely endearing himself to Tempest. He seemed to have lost that self-assurance he'd had only moments ago, she realized, and wondered if she was the cause for his sudden bout of nervousness. Instinct told her she was, and the knowledge secretly pleased her.

"I'm enrolled in the School of Architecture. And, uh, for my thesis I have to design and construct a scale model of my choice. Well, I've never been good at color and all that, so some friends of mine suggested that I check with an interior design student. And, well, that's when I heard about you."

All during the time that he spoke, Tempest's photographic mind clicked indelible pictures. He was casually dressed in a light blue plaid shirt with a white wool sweater tied around his wide shoulders. A pair of

23

faded jeans hugged his long legs to perfection, emphasizing his slender hips and muscular thighs.

Above all, it was his eyes that captured her.
They were coal black and set back under a hooded brow,
giving him a hawkish look. They snapped and glowed
when he spoke of his work, drawing her helplessly into
their inky depths with their intensity. His large hands
elicited strange feelings in the hollow of her stomach, as
she watched them drum on the tabletop as he spoke. He
was not handsome in the classical sense of the word, but
he exuded a raw sexual heat that scorched her like a
summer's day.

Braxton fidgeted uneasily in his chair, completely taken by Tempest's bold look compounded with her
seemingly easy manner. He became captivated by her
smile and throaty laughter. She was a maze of conflicts.
She gave the impression of being understated, yet she
had a wild and untamed look in her eyes that was barely held in check. Her long slender fingers looked fragile, but he felt deep within himself that those same hands
could ignite the embers that he knew he had yet to feel.
She made him feel powerful yet vulnerable. She made
him want to reach out and protect her fragile form. Yet
somehow he knew that she had the strength of will to
carry her through even the most difficult of life's obsta-
cles. How could one woman be so complex and simple,
wrapped into one breathtaking package? He knew that
he had to know her. He had to have her as his own.

What would those hands feel like stroking her

body, those lips pressed against hers, she wondered. She could feel the heat rise to her face and radiate downward to her center at the vision. Here she was, with a strange man, thinking such erotic thoughts. What would her grandmother think? Upstanding Ella Dailey would drop to her knees and throw up a prayer for Tempest's salvation, that's what, Tempest thought. Nonetheless, the sobering vision did not quell the growing response she felt for Braxton Thorne. She didn't think that anything could. Penetrating her thoughts, his voice drifted back to her.

"Actually...that's not true, either." He gave Tempest a sheepish grin. "I'd seen you around, like I said before. I guess I was just waiting for the right opportunity. Fortunately this thesis was it."

His eyes bore into hers, and her good senses left as she felt herself being swept away with his charm.

He wasn't even sure what he was saying to her. He knew only that he couldn't let this moment slip away.

"I don't usually do this kind of thing," he said, disarming her with that smile again.

"You mean pick up strange women?"

"You may be a lot of things, but strange isn't one of them."

His voice, as soothing as a lazy river, washed over her, drowning the last traces of resistance. Her unspoken decision startled her. At some point, she wasn't sure when, she had made up her mind that she wanted this man more than anything else.

Across the table their eyes were drawn in magnetic contact. In that brief second, an unspoken bond was created. Their eyes would become their secret weapons—have the power to unlock the doorways to their hearts, their souls.

They realized that power then, as they did now, drifting back together through a time that had never been forgotten, to a place where nothing was the same.

Over time she'd come to forgive him for the pain he'd caused her. Her anger had softened to a dull ache, exercised by the vehemence in which she drove herself. Still she knew deep within that if she would allow him to look into her eyes, her heart would be lost to him as it was so many springs ago. The realization of her vulnerability to him shook her. She couldn't allow that to happen, not now, not ever again.

She moved into the circle of David's arm and stood motionlessly by his side. The spell was broken, but her heart continued to thud uncontrollably in her chest. She heard David's voice, but didn't comprehend what he said until he ushered her into a seat nearest to him.

"Now that we have introductions out of the way, why don't we sit and get down to business. I'm sorry that I didn't mention to you earlier that my wife would be attending, but I wasn't sure if she would be able to make it. She returned from South America only last night."

"I couldn't have asked for a more exquisite surprise, Mr. Lang. Please don't apologize." He gave Tempest a pointed smile. She shifted uncomfortably in her seat, gave him the barest smile in response, and looked away.

✖✖✖

David looked questioningly on the static exchange but chose not to comment. Maybe she was still tired from her flight, he concluded. However, he pledged to get to the bottom of her unusual behavior before the day was out.

"Now that everyone is settled, I'll get the blueprints so that Mr. Thorne can get a sense of the layout. Tempest, why don't you show Mr. Thorne some of the sketches for the interior in the meantime."

In brisk, precise movements, David walked over to the built-in wall cabinets, pressed a hidden button, and the cabinet opened revealing rows of shelves stocked with drawings and blueprints. "My wife designed this office space also," David said over his shoulder.

Braxton turned to Tempest. "Impressive."

Tempest felt the heat rise to her face. She flipped open her portfolio determined to avoid Braxton's stare. But she couldn't avoid his nearness as he pulled his chair closer to hers. Having his body this close to her was almost more than she could stand.

From the corner of her eye, she saw the muscled thighs ripple against the obviously expensive tailor-made suit. He sported a full beard now, which only enhanced his masculinity, giving him a distinctive virile appeal. She wondered what it would feel like brushing against her skin. The vision caused a quake in her loins.

Stop it! Just stop it! she commanded herself. She had to pull herself together, and she couldn't just sit there in silence like some inane lump. David would be sure to think something was wrong. She cleared her throat.

"This is the design for the master bedroom."

He gave her a look that caused a tremor to run up her spine.

Just great, that would have to be the first picture.

"Here is the dining room, and this one is the first-floor bathroom."

"These are fabulous designs." He turned to look at her. "You're very talented, but I suppose you've been told that hundreds of times."

Coming from you, makes all the other comments bland in comparison. "I try to do my best." Her eyes met his. *What am I doing? My husband is less than ten feet away, and I'm practically in Braxton's arms. I can't let him do this to me again.* She averted her eyes just as David returned to the table with the layouts. He spread out the blueprints of the proposed complex and began explaining what had to be done.

"It's two thousand acres of space located on an

abandoned warehouse site in Bloomfield, New Jersey. There are thirty buildings in all. Each building has two stories, excluding the basements," he said, pointing to each of the buildings as he spoke. "They all have to be completely gutted. Plumbing, new steel beams, heating and air-conditioning units have to be installed. I'd like the project under way within the next month. Once the winter sets in, it will be extremely difficult to get any outside work done. What do you think, Mr. Thorne?"

"First, please call me Braxton." David nodded his assent. "Second, I'd like to know what was stored there before it was abandoned?"

"It was a munitions storehouse about fifteen years ago. Then it was bought out by a clothing manu-facturer to house surplus goods. The company, Bennington, Ltd., went bankrupt just over a year ago. That's when I bought it."

"So long as we don't have to worry about chem-ical waste coming back to haunt us. You have checked that out, I gather?"

"According to Ackerman Testing Company, the land is free of chemical waste. Ackerman is the best in the business."

"When can I get to see the site? I'll have a much better idea as to what needs to be done after I've seen the actual layout. I wouldn't feel comfortable giving you an answer until then."

"Of course. I can arrange to have someone take you out there by the middle of the week. How's that?"

"The sooner the better. Also, I'll need to see the soil sample reports from Ackerman."

"I have a copy here in the office. I'll have Annie get it for you before you leave." Then he turned to Tempest. "Tempest, if you're not busy, why don't you take Braxton out on Wednesday?"

Her mind raced for some excuse. She wasn't ready to be alone with Braxton.

"Uh, I'll really be tied up this week, David. With the Long Island estate under way, I really don't see where I'll have time. Perhaps I could get my assistant to go with Mr. Thorne. Bridgette knows the layout as well as I do, and she has a copy of the prints."

"But Bridgette isn't *you*. I'm sure—"

"I can't do it!" she snapped, barely maintaining control.

"Is something wrong? You've been acting rather peculiar since you arrived." David stepped around the table to her side, and put his hand on her shoulder. "You're not yourself today. Actually you look a bit ill."

"I'm sorry." She grasped the hand that held her shoulder and looked up into his eyes. "I guess it must be all the excitement of the trip and lack of sleep." She tried a smile that missed.

"I should apologize for getting you here so soon after your arrival. But you know I want you involved in this project from the beginning."

Braxton silently watched the intimate exchange, and his heart sank. Somehow he had convinced himself

30

that she couldn't possibly love David Lang. He just didn't seem her type. He almost laughed out loud at the thought. It had been a long time. He didn't know what her type was anymore. At one time it had been him. It nearly killed him when he read in *Interior Life* Magazine that she had married David Lang, and so soon after she left college. That, he never understood. Yet he knew that he had no one to blame but himself. He should have tried harder and not been dissuaded by her grandmother. He had let her get away, and now she belonged to someone else—someone who it was obvious that she deeply loved. It was also obvious to him that she wanted to continue to act as though she didn't know him. So if that was the way she wanted to play it, that's the way it would be. He was here to do a job, that was it, he weakly convinced himself. Just a job.

The sound of Tempest's voice floated to Braxton's ear, piercing through the shroud that had descended around his heart.

"I really can't take that trip out to Jersey, David. Please consider Bridgette."

"We'll discuss it later." His voice, cold and exact, ended any further discussion. He turned to Braxton. "I'll leave the rest of the details to you. I'm sure you are aware of the gravity of this project. With the continual upsurge in the shortage of affordable housing, this development would be manna from heaven for the community. So after you view the site, give me a call and we'll discuss contracts and start dates."

"I know an excellent contractor who could handle the construction, once I redesign the building to your specifications."

From there the three immersed themselves in deep conversation concerning the technical aspects of construction.

Tempest remained in body but her mind was far removed from the drawings and scale model in front of her. She heard the deep voices but she couldn't make out the words as her thoughts centered around this bizarre twist of fate. What in the world was she going to do? No way was she going to work with Braxton Thorne, promise to David or not. She couldn't, not after what Braxton had done, but most of all because of the way she still felt about him.

How could she explain that to David? She couldn't, of course, but she had to think of something. There was too much at stake for everyone.

"What do you think about that, Mrs. Lang?"

Was there a conversation going on? "I'm sorry—think about what?"

"Braxton suggested that the living room floor be dropped to give the dining area a European ambiance."

"I see." Tempest rose from her seat and walked to the other side of the table. "How long do you generally work on your plans before presentation, Mr. Thorne?"

Ugh-oh. "Months."

"So do I. Before I even dream of presenting my

designs to anyone, I go over every detail and dimension." She heard the shrillness in her voice but seemed unable to control it. "Do you realize the amount of work involved to incorporate your suggestion?"

"I didn't mean to imply that there was anything wrong with your designs."

"I'm sure that you didn't."

He flashed her an all-knowing smile that stopped her in her tracks.

What was she doing? Lashing out at Braxton was not going to solve anything. She was always short-sighted when it came to her work, but now was not the time to lose control. "I'm sure that you didn't," she said in a softer tone. "But I'm sure you can understand my concern."

"You must excuse my wife," David interjected. "She tends to be a bit overzealous when it comes to her work. That is one of the reasons why I tend to defer to her design decisions."

"You don't have to apologize for me, David." She smiled an apologetic smile. "I think I can handle that one myself." She turned to Braxton. "Please excuse me, Mr. Thorne. I do get a bit puffed up at times."

"No harm done," Braxton spun out in his soothing southern drawl. "Let's shake on it and start again." He extended his hand to her.

Oh, merciful heavens. The last thing she needed was to touch him, but it couldn't be avoided. She placed her hand in his and felt the heat of contact surge through

33

her body. He bent his head ever so slowly to plant a light kiss on her knuckle, his eyes never leaving hers. She drank in the heartrending tenderness of his gaze and knew that she was fast losing ground. A slight tremor shook her being when his lips met her burning flesh, and she quickly eased her hand away—but not before David caught the vaguely sensuous light that passed between them.

He stood by silently. An uneasy sensation crept through his veins at the seemingly innocent exchange. Perhaps he was wrong, but his instincts told him that he wasn't. There was more going on than what met the eye, and he was going to find out what it was. For the first time in more years than he cared to remember, he felt threatened. Threatened was something that David Lang would not tolerate. There was no way some architect would interfere with his plans. Tempest was the key to it all. He'd be damned if he'd let this man ruin it for him. As for Tempest, he'd deal with her as well.

David's icy voice effectively cut through the pulsating heat in the room. "I think that's about all we can do for now, Mr. Thorne. If you can get some preliminary drawings together for me by the end of the week, we'll meet again and set up the production schedule."

Braxton noticed the sharp change in David's attitude but chose to disregard it.

"Next week will be fine. I'll make that call to the contractor and see if I can meet with him to discuss the project."

Braxton gathered up the blueprints and looked at David.

David rose from his seat, meeting Braxton's eyes full on. A glint of challenge sparked in his dark brown eyes and tinged his voice.

"We'll be seeing each other soon then, Mr. Thorne." He gripped Braxton's hand in a crushing hold.

"Yes, we will," returned Braxton, with the same tone of resoluteness, not flinching under the grip, which incensed David all the more.

"My driver will take you to your hotel. I've made a reservation for you at the Hilton on Sixth Avenue. There will also be a car to pick up your associate, Mr. Hamilton, at the airport when he arrives this afternoon."

"You seem to have thought of everything. Thank you."

"I try to make the people I work with feel cared for," David said, flashing a private look in Tempest's direction. "I'm sure that my wife would vouch for me on that point." David pulled Tempest snugly against his side.

She nodded her assent and looked firmly at Braxton. "You'll find that as you work with David, he's a stickler for perfection. Everything has to be just right. Nothing is left to chance."

Braxton immediately caught the pointed look in her eyes and the subtle hint that underlined her innocent words.

"My wife knows me all too well." He gave Braxton a smug smile. "That happens after years of living and working so closely with someone." David's eyes burned into Braxton's, bringing his point home.

"I'm sure. In any case I'll be in touch during the week."

"Annie will show you out and give you the soil sample reports. She has your reservations, and the car is waiting downstairs to take you to your hotel."

"Thanks again. Mrs. Lang." Braxton extended his hand to Tempest. She took it and felt the heat race through her body once again.

"It was a pleasure to meet you at last," he continued. "I've been following your career for years."

Did his voice soften as he said that? Tempest's heart pounded in her chest. Had he really not forgotten her? Then why? She was more confused than ever, but there was nothing she could do about it. It was too late for them.

"I'm sure we'll meet again at some point, Mr. Thorne."

Was there more in her words than what she'd said? Then he saw it. In her eyes were the sparks of which he could have only dreamed. She still loved him. He was sure of it. It was all that he could do to keep from crossing the small space that separated them and sweeping her into his arms. He had to get her alone. They were somehow destined to be together. He would do anything in his power to see that happen, if only she were willing. Then the reality of her situation and his brought him plummeting back to earth. There was her husband to consider and his wife, Jasmine.

Braxton gave Tempest a brief nod and strode out of the office, crossing the invisible battlefield into the outer office. Tempest's heart raced as she sat down facing David. She knew she was in for a confrontation. He had an uncanny sixth sense when it came to her. She was sure that he intuitively felt her turmoil. She could not continue to keep up the front much longer, so she plunged right in, cutting him off before he began.

Rising from her seat she began to pace across the sienna-colored carpet. "Listen, David," she began. "I'm sorry to disappoint you, but I can't work on this project." She turned to face him, the huge glazed maple conference table separating them. She brushed past the standing ficus tree that graced one corner of the enormous office to stand next to her husband.

"What!" He nearly strangled on the word.

"I can't do it."

"Why in hell not? This is a golden opportunity for you and for me." He grabbed Tempest's shoulders, his well-manicured fingers boring into her as he spoke. "How many times in your career will you be offered something of this magnitude? This project will put your name on the map for good."

"I know that," she replied softly. She understood his confusion but was unable to explain. Instead

37

she pulled from his grasp to seek a safe haven on the other side of the table.

"It's too much of a commitment," she offered, searching desperately for a way out. "I have four other projects under my supervision. I can't afford to let my other clients suffer." She could never tell him the real reason.

He gently approached her and put a comforting arm around her stiff shoulders. "Listen," he said in his most patronizing tone, "why don't you think it over? Take a few days off and get your bearings. I'm sure Bridgette could handle some of the load—ask her. Then we'll talk again. How—"

"Stop it! Just stop it," she said, pulling away from him. "You can't keep treating me like a child!"

"Then stop acting like one!"

"I know what I can and cannot do. And *you* cannot continue to manipulate my life, David."

"Manipulate your life? Is that what you think this is all about?"

She immediately regretted her outburst, seeing the pained look in his eyes. She didn't want to hurt David, but she couldn't tell him the truth.

"I've got to go, David. I have a full day ahead of me. I'll think it over, but I doubt if I'll change my mind." She turned to leave.

"I'm your husband, Tempest." His steely voice stopped her in her tracks. She spun to face him. "I was the one you came running to. I was the one who got your business off the ground. I demand an explanation—a better one than you've given me. You owe me!"

"So you finally said it," she whispered in a voice rimmed with pain. "Owe you. That's what it's all about, isn't it?"

"Tempest, please, I'm sorry. You know I didn't mean that." David quickly saw everything that he had dreamed about slipping through his fingers. "Why don't we wait until we've both calmed down and talk about this later, when I return. I love you, you know that." He pulled her into his arms, his mouth only a breath away from hers. "It's been rough on the both of us. We need to get away, to be alone, just the two of us." He pulled her still closer.

Tempest weakened. Maybe David was right. After her ordeal today, she did need to get away. Perhaps there was hope for them, if she would allow Braxton to get out of her system.

"I'll think about it, David. I won't make any promises. But you're right, we do need to spend some time together."

"I knew you'd see it my way." His mouth swept down on hers, demanding, urgent. For one brief moment, she let her body succumb, as *his* face, Braxton's face, floated before her eyes—then reality replaced the barest moment of illusion. She gently eased herself from his hold.

"I've really got to go. I'll see you when you get back."

"I'll be working late at the office when I return. I'll send a car for you."

"Fine, I'll see you then." Tempest gave him a quick kiss on the cheek, picked up her belongings, and left the office.

David stared pensively out of the window, his hands gripping the ledge, his finely chiseled features a mask of fury. He had a plan. Returning to his desk he punched on the intercom.

"Yes, Mr. Lang?"

"Get Marty Jackson on the phone."

"The private detective?"

"You heard me. Do it now, and put him right through when you reach him."

"Yes, Mr. Lang."

"And another thing, Annie, don't ever question me again." He released the button before Annie could respond and waited for the phone to ring.

※

On the ride down the elevator, hundreds of thoughts tumbled through her head. She couldn't take this job—not if she had to work with Braxton. He was sure to find out. But was she really prepared to jeopardize her career that she had struggled so hard to attain for a show of pride? She wasn't sure. She knew only that in just the short space of time that she'd been with Braxton, she was completely unglued. To think that after all of this time he could still have such an unsettling effect on her emotions left her totally shaken. She had to think, but she couldn't. Her head began to pound with the effort.

Stepping out into the balmy spring air, she strolled aimlessly through the crowd of early lunchgoers. She plowed through the surging traffic, oblivious to the blaring horns, ignoring the red lights, and curses of the irate drivers. On the corner of Fiftieth Street and Madison Avenue, she hailed a cab.

"One World Trade Center," she ground out between clenched teeth, slamming the door behind her as if the driver were the source of her quandary.

Settling back in the speeding cab, she envisioned the stack of mail, messages, problems, smiling faces, and innumerable questions that would confront her. She massaged her temples. Her head throbbed. She couldn't handle it, she decided. Not today.

"Driver, I've changed my mind. Make that Twenty-third and Seventh. Sorry," she added in a more congenial tone.

Maybe a long hot bath and some sleep would clear her head and calm her nerves. Her "Gram" firmly believed that sleep and a hot bath would cure anything.

What she needed more than anything right then was to be alone with her thoughts. But visions of Braxton continued to intrude on her—hovering patiently, waiting to leap on her as soon as she let her guard down. Then with shocking clarity she realized the extraordinary void that she'd felt when he had walked out of David's office. As much as she tried to fight what she felt, seeing him again was the first time she'd felt whole in too many years.

Chapter Three

The heavy brocade drapes remained drawn, encasing the finely furnished suite in comforting darkness. Braxton, still fully clothed, sat limp on the edge of his hotel bed completely immobilized after seeing Tempest. The last few hours had left him drained. He rubbed his hand across his bearded cheeks and stared intently at the bedside phone. He willed the phone to ring, but he knew that of course it would not.

Why would she call him after all this time? She'd never tried in all these years. That stark reality still ate at him.

With a deep sigh of resignation, he pulled himself up from the bed and paced the heavily carpeted floor. But his eyes kept drifting back to the phone. Several times he was involuntarily propelled in its direction. He fought down the urge to call her office. Still taunting urgings whispered in his head. It was only a matter of looking up the number in the phone book. After all, they did have to work together.

His better judgment overruled. No, not twice in one day. Just seeing each other after all this time was enough of a jolt for both of them. He couldn't put her through anything more. At least he'd been prepared. She was obviously stunned by the look she'd had on her face.

That thought triggered another. Her husband's whole change in attitude was needling him. Did he know about his and Tempest's past? If so, then why was Tempest pretending not to know him? He shook his head in bewilderment. Then his thoughts were interrupted by an insistent buzzing. Realizing that it was the door, he crossed the room in long, brisk strides, sure that it was room service. Opening the door, he couldn't have been happier to see anyone else at that moment. "Compliments of the house, sir." Standing at the door with a wide grin and outstretched arms was his partner and boyhood friend, Scott Hamilton. The two men embraced as Braxton ushered Scott into the suite.

"Where are your bags? They didn't get lost, did they?"

"Naw. The bellhop is right behind me."

As if on cue, the bellhop deposited the bags inside the suite. Braxton shooed away Scott's attempt to give the young man a tip and instead dug into his pocket and produced a five dollar bill.

"Thank you, sir!" With an effusive smile he quickly pocketed the money and made a hasty exit.

"Well, you're sure in a generous mood," quipped Scott. "But you look like hell." Scott plopped down in the first available seat and kicked off his size eleven shoes.

"Thanks. You always were good for my ego."

"I take it you saw her?"

"I saw her all right."

"So are you going to tell me what happened, or do I have to beat it out of you?"

Braxton smiled for the first time in hours. Maybe talking it out with Scott would help him to put things in perspective. Scott had always been the practical one, and he sure needed some practical advice now. Taking a seat opposite Scott, Braxton spun out the events of the morning.

"I still don't get it though, Scott. He just isn't her type. He has to be at least ten years older than her."

"Maybe she has a thing for older men now." Scott winked and poked Braxton in the rib, hoping to lighten the mood.

Braxton shook his head. "It's more than that. He's the pompous sort, real full of his own importance. It doesn't seem that he has a warm bone in his body."

"Maybe that's what you wanted to see."

"No. I know that's not it. She still cares, Scott. I saw it. Only for a minute, but I saw it in her eyes." He looked to Scott for reassurance of his beliefs.

Scott reached out and patted Braxton's shoulder.

"Maybe she does. But what good is it going to do? She's married and so are you."

"Jasmine and I have been separated for two years."

"That doesn't change the fact that she has refused to divorce you."

Braxton sprang up from his seat, jammed his hands in his pockets, and began to pace again.

"She has to divorce me. There's nothing holding us together anymore. I've paid her back the money that her father loaned me when my father died, in more ways than one. There's no love between us. There never was, except maybe in the beginning." He gave a poor imitation of a laugh.

"My marriage was probably the biggest mistake I've made beside letting Tempest get away."

Scott stood up and grabbed Braxton by the shoulders. "That wasn't all your fault, B.J. She had a role in it, too. She told her grandmother to tell you that she didn't want to see you anymore. You had a lot on you—your father's death for one. His business was going under. You had to sell the house to pay off his debts, then find someplace else to live. What were you supposed to do? I know Jasmine has turned out to be a real bitch, but at least she was there."

Braxton pulled away from Scott's hold. "Yeah, she was there, but she had her reasons, too. You know that as well as I do! Then between her drinking and her affairs—"

"Okay, okay, you're right." He put up his hand in mock defense. "Don't get bent out of shape. Let's just say you do get your divorce, what happens then? What makes you think that Tee will leave her husband?"

"I just know she will," he said in a hoarse whisper. "We were meant to be together. I know it. I feel it in my gut."

"Listen," Scott said gently. "I know how much you love her. I was there, remember?"

Braxton flashed him a knowing smile.

"I just don't want to see you hurt like that again. Take it one step at a time."

"I just need to get her alone and talk with her. Fate has given us a second chance. If I blow it this time, I'll never find peace within myself."

That familiar light ignited in Braxton's eyes, and Scott knew that the old Braxton was finally back. He was just glad that he would be there for the fireworks as he was sure there would be.

"I'm not going to give up this time. I'm going to get some answers and hopefully Tempest in the process. All I know is that I have to try."

"I've been waiting six years to hear you say that." Scott gave Braxton a thumbs-up sign. A look of friendly challenge sparked in his eyes. "So what's the holdup?" He tipped his hand in the direction of the phone. "Start dialing."

Braxton, needing no further encouragement,

walked to the phone, picked it up, and dialed information.

✖✖✖

The cab pulled up in front of Tempest and David's loft apartment building. Maybe she could steal a few moments of solitude and clear her head before Clara brought Kai home from school.

As she stuck her key in the door, she was still amazed with the transformation her body took when she stepped off the crowded pollution-filled street and into the tranquility of their loft.

Entering into the cool pastels was like taking off tight shoes after a long day. Tempest let out a deep sigh of satisfaction, as she switched on the lights bathing the entrance foyer in a soft glow that bounced and reflected off of the high-gloss wood floors. Hanging her blazer on the brass coat rack, she ascended onto the raised platform that was her living room.

It had taken her almost two years to get the layout of the loft completed, she thought with a degree of pride. The copper-colored couch was covered in a rich damask fabric, and it took up three-quarters of the platform, leaving enough room to enter and exit and space to contain a small bar.

Tempest fixed herself a glass of wine, switched on the stereo, and curled up on the couch. The bath would have to wait, she decided, reaching over to the cordless telephone. *First I'd better call the office. Bridgette will be sending out the National Guard any minute now.*

The office phone was picked up on the first ring. Her secretary answered.

"Hi, Marsha, it's me. Tell Bridgette I won't be in today. I'm <u>exhausted</u>. It's been a trying morning. She'll have to handle the natives one more day."

"I'm sure she won't mind," quipped Marsha. "You know how she enjoys being in charge."

"Do I have any messages?"

"Only one. A Mr. Thorne called."

Tempest's heart stopped. Marsha heard the quick intake of breath.

"Ms. Dailey, are you all right?"

"Yes. Ah, the wine must have gone down the wrong way. What did he want?"

"Actually he was very <u>insistent</u> that I give him your home number. He said he had some details he wanted to go over with you as soon as possible. Something to do with that new project, but I told him I wasn't allowed to give out that information. Did I do the right thing? It can wait until you come in, can't it? I know how you like to handle the major projects yourself, so I told him to stop by tomorrow if it was that important."

"You what?" Tempest screeched, trying to control her rising panic.

"I told him to come in tomorrow. Did I do something wrong? He said——"

"No, no, you did the right thing. I'm sorry. I guess I'm just overtired," she added, hoping to cover up her inexcusable outburst. "Did he say anything? I mean, did he say what time he'd be at the office?" She was falling apart and she knew it. She just hoped that Marsha didn't.

"Nine-thirty. Is that too early? I told him you usually get in early, so it would be all right."

"Nine-thirty?"

"If it's too early, I could call and reschedule. He left his number."

"He did? I mean, nine-thirty is fine. I'll see you tomorrow." She didn't wait for Marsha to hang up but absently laid the phone on the floor.

She didn't have time to think about the implications of a private meeting with Braxton. Clara and Kai had just returned home earlier than expected.

Kai came running into the living room when she saw the lights.

"Mommy, what are you doing home? You said you had to go to work."

"I know, sweetie." She gave Kai a hug. "But I had a very hectic morning. I decided to come home early. Is that okay with you?" she asked with a smile.

"Sure! Can you take me to the park?"

"After you finish your homework."

"Yeah!"

"Now go wash your hands, miss," Clara

instructed. "I'll fix you a snack."

"Goodie!" Kai raced off in the direction of the bathroom, ponytail swinging.

Clara stood over the reclining Tempest. "You want to tell me what you're really doing here?"

"I can't talk about it now, Clara. Maybe later."

"Well, I'm here if you need to talk."

"Thanks." Tempest curled up further into the cushiony couch.

"Will David be home for dinner?"

"Not tonight," she said, pointedly avoiding Clara's penetrating gaze. "He has to go out of town."

"Did the two of you get things settled?"

Tempest flipped open a magazine from the coffee table and feigned indifference. "We didn't have time. We're going out to dinner tomorrow. We'll talk then."

"Good." Clara moved toward the kitchen and then stopped. "By the way, how did the new architect work out?"

"I'm sure he'll be just fine," she mumbled.

"Was he anyone you were familiar with?"

Familiar! She almost laughed, but instead the pent-up tears slowly rolled down her cheeks.

"Honey, what's wrong?" Clara hurried to her side.

"Oh, Clara. It's Braxton."

Clara cradled Tempest's head against her ample bosom. "What do you mean?"

51

"Braxton." She sniffed. "He's the architect that David hired."

Clara's eyes rose upward as she sighed. "Oh, honey, it's all right," she soothed. "Get it all out." She pulled Tempest into the comfort of her arms and rocked her.

"Clara, it was so good to see him and so painful. Why did he leave me? I needed him so much, Clara. Why?" She yielded to the compulsive sobs that shook her.

Clara held on to her, feeling so helpless. Watching this child whom she loved as her own suffer was so acute, it was like a physical pain. She searched for words, knowing that none would suffice.

"I can't answer that for you. All I do know is that everything happens for a reason, even if we don't understand what those reasons are. Maybe now is the time to finally put it all to rest once and for all."

"It"s not that simple." Tempest whipped a hand across her tear-streaked face and took a deep cleansing breath. "You don't know the half of it."

"Maybe I don't. I don't need to. But finding out what happened between the two of you may finally help you to put your mind at rest and go on with your life the best you can."

"Maybe." But her heart squeezed in anguish as she believed that knowing why wasn't going to change anything. Not now.

"In the meantime, dry your eyes." Clara pulled

a handkerchief from her pocket and handed it to Tempest. "Kai will be back any minute."

"Thanks, Clara." She sniffed back the last traces of tears. "What in the world am I going to do? The company could really use this publicity, and we worked so hard. But I can't possibly work with him." She looked up imploringly at Clara.

"I'm sure you'll make the right decision. You always do."

If you only knew.

Kai skipped back into the room. "Miss Clara, can I have my snack now? I'm hungry."

"Aren't you always? Well, come with me to the kitchen and we'll check those hands under the light." Clara gave Tempest an encouraging smile over her shoulder, then hustled Kai off to the kitchen.

Wearily Tempest rose from the couch and went to her room. In mechanical movements she changed into jeans, a sweatshirt, and a pair of sneakers for her romp in the park with her daughter.

The hour in the park, swinging on the swings and chasing Kai around the baseball field, gave Tempest the lift she desperately needed. Kai's constant chatter and earsplitting giggles temporarily took her mind off her troubles. They were both exhausted when they returned.

"Dinner will be ready in about thirty minutes," Clara called from the kitchen.

"Yeah! We're starved. Right, Mommy?"

Her answering smile reflected the adoration she had for her daughter. "Right. Now let's get you in the tub before dinner."

✂

Dinner completed, Tempest sat beside Kai as she said her prayers, then tucked her securely in bed.

"Good night, sweetie." Tempest placed a light kiss on Kai's lips.

"'Night, Mommy." Kai yawned. "Mommy, how come you look so unhappy today?"

She doesn't miss a trick. "I guess I'm still a little tired from my trip." How many times could that excuse be used, she wondered.

"Oh." Kai's eyes drifted close. "I said a special prayer for you."

"What was that?"

"That you get your real smile back." Kai rolled over and slipped off to sleep.

Tempest sat there momentarily shaken. She couldn't let this affect Kai. She'd spent too many years trying to make things right for her. Gently she rose from the bed, switched off the light, and left the room.

Clara was standing outside Kai's door. "Is there anything I can get you before I turn in?"

"No, thanks."

"Are you feeling any better?"

"Not really. But I'll be all right." She patted Clara's shoulder. "I'm going to take a shower and turn in early."

"That's probably best. Things always look better in the morning."

"I hope so."

✕⌒✕

When she'd finished her shower, she found a glass of warm milk laced with honey on her bedside table. That was just like Clara, she thought with a smile.

She put on her favorite scent, *Eternity*, slipped on a pale blue, floor-length gown and slid between the sheets. But two hours later, even after the warm milk, she was wide awake. Her mind would not let her rest. Braxton filled her mind and her soul as powerfully as if he lay beside her.

She wished that she could at least feel resentment or anger, something that she could use to defend against the force of her emotions for him. But she couldn't. As much as she hated to admit it, she was as much at fault as he was. She could have waited. She could have returned to Virginia to find him. She could have. Oh, what difference did it make? She did what she had to—do the right thing—the same thing any respectable, well-brought up young woman would have

55

done. And she would do the right thing now.

She'd stay with her husband and once and for all put Braxton out of her life, even at the expense of losing this job. Even at the expense of her own happiness.

She twisted and turned under the covers. She had to get some sleep. She had a big day tomorrow.

Tomorrow, she thought wearily. Tomorrow meant seeing him again—and tomorrow was too soon, much too soon.

Chapter Four

Arriving earlier than usual at her office, Tempest tried to mentally prepare herself for the ordeal ahead. The soft pastels that embraced her lacked the comfort and tranquility that they normally held for her. Her sleepless night had left her tense, as visions of Braxton had surrounded her, leaving her unable to find the peace that she sought in sleep.

She had to pull herself together, she knew, as she busied herself with watering the countless plants in her office. She could not let Braxton know the shattering effect his reappearance had on her. Yet everywhere that she turned, his face assaulted her. His scent swam through her senses, leaving her breathless and shaky. It would be so easy to succumb to him, so easy to let him touch her heart.

Tossing aside the thoughts which threatened to enslave her, she took a seat on the low sleek couch and thumbed through some of the patterns and wall coverings that would be needed for the new wing of the estate on the Long Island Sound. Before she knew it, she was completely engrossed in what she loved, planning the layout of a new project. It wasn't until the sound of the intercom intruded on her that she realized how much time had passed.

Her heart quickened when she checked her watch and stepped toward her desk. *Please don't let it be him, not yet,* she prayed.

"Yes, Marsha?" she said, depressing the button as the red light flashed on her desk phone. Her pulse pounded wildly in her ears.

"Is there anything you need for your meeting this morning? Should I send out for breakfast?"

There's something I need, she thought. *New insides.*

"Some coffee will be fine," she replied instead, thankful for the momentary reprieve. "Has Bridgette arrived yet?"

"She just came in."

"Good. When she gets settled, ask her if she would come in."

"Yes, Ms. Dailey."

Tempest clicked off. Moving toward the windows that spanned the length of one side of the room, she twirled the wand of the vertical blinds, emitting a warm peach glow that slid across the spacious room. Looking down the thirty stories to the ground, Tempest lost herself in the life that bloomed below. From all corners, people converged on the Towers. The busy streets throbbed with vitality. Tempest felt the energy that was barely held in check, and wondered with growing alarm if Braxton was among the pulsating crowd. Pushing back the vision, she tore her eyes away from the swarming masses, just as Bridgette's bubbling voice overflowed into the solitude of her office.

"You rang, your majesty?" Bridgette quipped, flashing a quick smile and extending a cup of steaming black coffee.

Turning, Tempest faced her dearest friend, and the smile that was ever ready on Bridgette's stunning face was instantly replaced with worry.

"Are you all right?" Concern spanned her face as she placed the coffee-filled cup on the desk. "You look like you've seen a ghost."

"Almost," Tempest said, attempting a smile that missed. "I need to talk. Do you have a few minutes?"

"For you, anytime. The way you look, my client will just have to wait. So talk." Bridgette took a seat on the opposite side of Tempest's mahogany desk and took a sip of her coffee.

"He's back."

"Who?" But before Tempest could answer, she realized just who *he* was. "Braxton?"

A bare nod was her reply.

"Oh, no, Tempest." Her heart reached out to her friend, seeing her pain and confusion. "What are you going to do?"

"Do? I'm going to stay as far away from him as I can. That's what I'm going to do," she stated flatly, attempting a bravado that she did not feel.

Of all the people in Tempest's life, Bridgette was the only other person beside Tempest's grandmother that she had entrusted with her secret. But only Bridgette knew the hidden loneliness and the struggle that Tempest had fought with over the years trying to get over Braxton Thorne. She also knew that she never won that battle. As much as Tempest had protested the fact, Bridgette knew better. Her heart had never let Braxton go.

"I take it you've seen him," she said softly, gently trying to lift the cloud that descended over Tempest's eyes.

"He's the architect that David hired for the housing complex."

"How in the world did David find Braxton, of all people?"

"You know David," Tempest said sardonically. "He always has to have the best. Unfortunately Braxton is just that—at least under the circumstances. David would go to hell and back if he thought it would get him what he wanted."

"I guess you would be the one to know," Bridgette said, then quickly realized her mistake when she saw the storm clouds brewing behind Tempest's hazel eyes. "Sorry. I didn't mean it the way it sounded. I just mean...well...you are married to the man."

"Married is the operative word here. That's why I'm not taking the job," she stated defiantly, crossing her arms across her chest.

"What? Not taking the job. Are you crazy?" Bridgette sprang up from her seat.

"There's no way that I'm going to work with David and Braxton. I suggested to David that you handle the project, but he is totally against it."

"That job could mean millions to the company. Did you think about that, while you were mapping out our future?" Bridgette's usual even temperament was quickly disappearing at her friend's illogical reasoning.

"If you're over him like you say you are, then what's the big deal about working with him?" Bridgette probed, digging for the real reason which she knew lay just beneath the surface. But she wanted her friend to face the truth for herself.

Had it been anyone else who said that to her, Tempest would have exploded, but she knew Bridgette always meant well, even if she was a bit outspoken at times.

An assortment of emotions flitted across Tempest's coppery face. What finally remained was pure and simple, stubborn pride. It rose to the surface and carved itself on her sculpted features.

Bridgette recognized that look, and a shudder ran through her veins. Pride is what carried Tempest through those trying times. It was all that she had, no matter how supportive Bridgette had been. She held on to it like a drowning man hanging on to driftwood. It would take more than the loss of a job to snatch that pride away from her. The gravity of the situation gripped her. She searched frantically for a way to get through to her friend. She had to make her see that she could not keep running from Braxton forever.

Tempest turned to stare out onto the street below. Couldn't Bridgette, of all people, see what this decision was doing to her? She had mistakenly expected her to understand. Obviously, she couldn't.

"We have plenty of business to carry us over, with or without the complex." Her tone brooked no argument. She turned to face Bridgette.

"Fine. If that's the way you want it." Velvet brown eyes challenged hazel. "Just how long do you think it will be before he finds out? It's time, Tempest. Time to face yourself and each other." Her tone softened as she saw the effect her words had on Tempest. "You can't keep running forever." She wanted to reach out and wipe away the hurt that still hung heavy behind the facade of control, but she knew that her efforts would be futile. Instead she turned to go, realizing that Tempest would have to deal with the situation the best way she could. Bridgette only hoped that she would finally do the right thing.

"I have an appointment in fifteen minutes. I'd better go."

The only sound in the stifling silence that followed was the swish of Bridgette's suede skirt as her long strides carried her across the office and out, closing the door gently behind her. She didn't know how long she stood there, soaking in what Bridgette said. Her decision was the right one. Wasn't it?

She didn't know anymore. All she knew for sure was that she couldn't risk her heart to Braxton again. Risk it she would if she went through with this project.

Heavy with indecision, she slumped down into her high-back leather chair, shifting and reshifting the papers on her desk.

As Bridgette stormed past Marsha on her way out she crashed with a thud into long hard muscle, knocking the breath completely out of her. Strong hands gripped her waist, keeping her from losing her balance. A velvety voice drifted to her subconscious.

"I guess I wasn't looking where I was going," the voice chuckled. "Are you all right, pretty lady?"

Bridgette's gaze rose from the broad chest and sunk into the unfathomable darkness that were his eyes. For a split second that could have been an eternity, she couldn't speak. To her ears, her voice sounded as if it were coming from under water when she responded.

"I—I'm fine. Thanks." Her knees turned to jelly when the roguish smile enveloped her. "It was really my fault," she muttered inanely.

"I see she has you all riled up, too," he drawled, the lift of his bearded chin pointing in the direction of Tempest's office.

In a flash of recognition, it finally sank in who

this devilishly handsome man was.

Straightening up and slipping from his grasp, Bridgette stood her ground, virtually accusing him with her look.

"Are you here to see Ms. Dailey?" Her protective instincts rose to her friend's defense, as if her slight frame could stop him.

"If it's all right with you," he answered smoothly, stripping away her guard with a brilliant grin.

She felt herself slip back into the gentle hold of his charm, but she quickly regained her balance.

"Perhaps I can help you. I'm her assistant, Bridgette Morgan."

"It would be nice if you could, pretty lady, but Tempest is the one I'm here to see. So if you'll excuse me." He brushed past her and stopped at Marsha's desk.

"Please tell Ms. Dailey that Braxton Thorne is here to see her."

Marsha pressed down on the intercom while Bridgette stood by helplessly. *No wonder Tempest never got over him*, she thought, her own pulse still racing.

Tempest jumped at the sound of the buzz from her phone. This time she knew it would be Braxton. Drawing on all of her strength, she surprised herself at how steady her voice sounded.

"Yes, Marsha?"

"Mr. Thorne is here."

"I'll be with him in a few minutes." She

released the button, taking a deep breath at the same time. Carving a path in the coral-colored carpet, she mentally ticked off the seconds. *How long can I make him wait*, she worried. *Until my heart stops thundering in my chest. Which may be never when it comes to him.* Knowing Braxton, if she waited too long, he'd just come bursting in there anyway. She couldn't let him come strolling in and see her with anxiety spelled out all over her face. She felt like a silly schoolgirl on her first date instead of a thirty-two-year-old executive. She quickly took a seat behind the desk. At least the desk could hide her trembling knees. Willing her heart to be still, she signaled to Marsha that she could show Mr. Thorne in.

His large frame took up the opened doorway. He was resplendent in an off-white linen jacket, burgundy silk shirt, left open just enough to expose the silken hairs on his broad chest, and black linen slacks that barely hid the bulging muscles of his thighs.

Tempest's insides dissolved and ran through her veins like rivers of fire at the sight of him. Sensations that she was sure were dead and buried rose with such blinding intensity that she thought for sure she would succumb to the ever growing flame that burned hotter by the minute. But she held on to the last bit of sanity she had, dousing the flame with a bucket of sheer will.

"Come in, Braxton. I understand that you have business to discuss with me." Rising from behind her desk, she stood to face him.

Where was the determination that he had only moments ago? It seemed to slip away at the sight of her. *She is magnificent*, he thought, *wild and untamed set in the perfect backdrop for her turbulent personality.*

⚜

Plants abounded everywhere—standing, hanging, and draping themselves over low glass tables. It was as though he were transported to a tropical paradise, in the middle of the bustling, chaotic city. The muted peach and deeper coral tones of the office gave off a soothing tranquility that belied the static atmosphere reverberating in the momentary silence.

She stood out in her tropical paradise like a goddess, covered in a lightweight pale green, cotton suit. Her near-sheer blouse revealed just enough of the swollen loveliness beneath to set his heart racing. Her skirt, coming just above her knees, called out to him to stroke the unbelievably long legs that glided effortlessly toward him. Did she realize what she was doing to him? Obviously not, by the strictly business tone she took with him.

"Let's sit over here," she said, indicating a smaller conference table with the tilt of her slender hand. She wasn't sure how she made it to the other side of the room, with her knees threatening to give out any minute. Somehow she did.

"Now what was it you wanted to discuss with

me?"

So that's the way she wants to play it. Well, this time she's in for a surprise.

"I'm not here on business, Tempest," he stated bluntly. "You're going to hear me out whether you want to or not."

Tempest's heart thudded. The churning sensation in her stomach made her light-headed as she sprang from her seat.

"Everything was said between us a long time ago. I don't see——"

Braxton jumped up and grabbed her shoulders, swinging her around to face him. His breath was hot on her cheek. The manly scent of him clouded her vision. She wanted to pull away, but the strength of his grip left her helpless, weak in the knees, as the heat of their intimate contact took her breath away. How easy it would be to collapse in his arms, forget the commitment she'd made to herself, and simply give in to him. But she could not. There was too much at stake.

"Let go of me, Braxton." Her eyes caught the rays of the morning sun, giving them a dangerous glint.

"Not until you sit down and listen to me." The easy manner was gone. In its place was an audible tenacity that shook her with its force. The look in his eyes melted her resolve. She never felt herself slip into the chair beneath her, until the back of her legs brushed against the chrome finish.

"That's better. You can't keep running from

me."

How many times would she hear that in one day? The rising panic was making her giddy. She struggled for control.

"What makes you think I'm running? There's nothing—"

"There's everything, and you know it. What we had was something beautiful. I know I had my faults. I admit that. But they weren't anything that we couldn't have worked out together. It had to be more than that. All I want to know is, what was it? What happened to us, to our plans?"

"What was I supposed to think, Braxton? You walked out on me, on us." She jumped up from her seat and shot him an accusing look. "Remember?" Her temper rose as the old wounds opened, fresh, stinging.

He was stunned into silence. He remembered. Every day of his life he remembered, but he'd come to terms with his mistakes. It was time that she did as well. "Why did you do it, Tempest? Why did you marry David Lang? I want...I need to know."

The buzzing intercom gave her a brief reprieve. "Yes, Marsha?"

"Mrs. Washington needs to speak with you immediately about the fabrics for the estate. She sounds more impatient than usual."

"Thank you. I'll call her right back." She looked up at Braxton. A tense silence enveloped the room, as she witnessed the anxiety behind those ebony

68

eyes. *Oh God, what can I say to him? I can't tell him. It is too late.* With every ounce of will that she had left, she strung out the words that ripped at her very soul.

"I have a life now," she said flatly. Rising she walked toward the window. She kept her back to him. "There's no room for you in it."

He felt his heart twist inside his chest. This was worse than he could have imagined. He wanted to reach out and grab her. But the pain of her words left him immobile. Instead he reached out to her with his soul, hoping to touch a place within her that had not turned to ice.

"Can you be that unfeeling, so unforgiving, after all that we meant to each other? Don't I at least deserve an explanation? Is there no compassion left in you? What happened to the caring woman that I knew?" He watched her shoulders stiffen at those last words.

She's still here, she thought, as tears threatened to overflow. *She's locked up inside a fortress, hiding from feelings that she cannot control when it comes to you.*

"I think you'd better leave."

"You may be able to pretend to forget me, Tempest, push me to the back of your mind. But you know as well as I do that we still love each other. Nothing you can say or do is going to convince me that what you felt for me is not still there, just as it is for me. Don't ever forget that, *stormy one.*" With that he snatched up his briefcase, giving one parting look at the figure that refused to face him, and swung away toward the door.

The instant that he left, Tempest felt the heavy pressure of his absence. The room lost its vibrancy, the air ceased to move. For countless seconds she remained absolutely motionless, until a shudder of pure despair ran through her. The tears which she had refused to shed ran helplessly down her high cheeks. She spun toward the door, her mind screaming his name. But he was gone.

The words he spoke struck back at her like bolts of lightning. He'd called her *stormy one*. The simple words forced fresh tears to run. It had been his pet name for her in their deepest moments of intimacy, she recalled. Moments buried, she reminded herself. Or were they? She couldn't trust her emotions any longer.

Moving to shut the open door, she thought of the barrage of questions that he had thrown out to her. She'd been so wrapped up in shutting him out, that she hadn't really listened. What did he mean when he said that it had to be more than his fault? She didn't have time to think further, when the ringing of her private line interrupted her thoughts. She cleared her throat, picked up the phone, and took a deep breath, trying to resume her shaken presidential poise.

"Tempest Dailey," she stated simply.

"Tempest, it's David." His clipped voice grated on her raw nerves. "I'm calling to confirm dinner tonight." For a brief moment, she'd forgotten her promise to David. Now she desperately wanted a way out, but could find no viable excuse.

"Did you have any place in mind?"

"I thought Jezebel's would be perfect. We had a lot of pleasant times there." His voice hinted at more than his words revealed.

"So long as we can just relax. No heavy discussions, David. I'm not in the mood."

"You sound a bit tense. Is something wrong?"

"Nothing's wrong." She held back a sigh that hung on her lips.

"I'll have a car pick you up at the loft at seven-thirty. I've made reservations for eight."

"Seven-thirty is fine. I'll see you then." She let the phone drop back in the cradle. Breathing deeply, she tried to shake off the effects of the past half-hour and focus on the tasks at hand. Work had been her only salvation for years, and she sought its protective shield again.

Pulling her hair behind her shoulder, she thumbed through her phone book and located Mrs. Washington's number. After fifteen minutes of nonstop chatter, she finally gave Tempest her billionth instruction about the bedroom fabrics and wall coverings.

With that unpleasant task aside, Tempest flipped open her huge plan book and immersed herself in the details of running her design firm. But the realities of her personal life clung to her like morning dew, willing her to come to terms with that aspect of her life as well.

Chapter Five

The morning flew by without any other major interruptions. Tempest had completed the monthly project report and outlined the items still to be attended.

After hours of huddling over her desk, she finally stood up and stretched her tight muscles. With that aside, the stark reality of her situation ignited anew. No longer having the distraction of her work, the scenes of the morning returned in full force. There was no way she could avoid coming to grips with her life. Bridgette was right, and so was Braxton, she resignedly admitted. Still a part of her was not willing or able to relinquish the tight hold she had on her emotions.

There has to be another way, she thought, absently stroking a standing palm tree near the window. She certainly could not afford to let this job go. She would have to think of something. In the meantime business must go on.

Gathering up her purse and her sketches of the Long Island estate, she headed out of her office. Stopping briefly at Marsha's desk, she explained that she would be out of the office for the balance of the day, shopping for fabric.

"What time will you be in tomorrow, Ms. Dailey?"

"Early as usual, I'm afraid," Tempest said, giving Marsha a half-smile. "I have a lot of catching up to do."

"See you in the morning."

"If you need me for anything," Tempest called over her shoulder, "leave a message on my machine. I'll check periodically. Just in case I miss you here."

"Certainly, Ms. Dailey."

⌘

Back at the hotel Braxton discussed the layout of the housing complex with Scott. The elegant hotel suite had been transformed into a temporary office. Rented drafting tables, gooseneck lamps, and rolls of drawings took up half of one side of the spacious quarters. The two friends poured over their work, while debating the right approach to take.

Since his early morning meeting with Tempest, Scott was acutely aware of the dramatic change in Braxton. He had refused to discuss the meeting but instead immersed himself into his work. Although he appeared to be interested in the work before him, his mind was obviously elsewhere, as many times Scott caught the faraway look in Braxton's eyes. As much as he wanted to know what had happened, he felt it best to let him open up on his own. Maybe what they needed was a change in atmosphere, he thought, although Scott sensed that the problem lay deeper.

"Listen, B.J., why don't we take a break from all of this? We've been working nonstop for hours, and I could use a hot shower and a good meal. What do you say?"

Scott was one of the few people that he let call him B.J. Anything was better than junior, he'd decided years ago, but between close friends, Braxton often sounded too formal.

"You go on. I think I'll just stay here and try to work out these calculations for the room dimensions."

With a short sigh, Scott rose from the table, stretching his lithe, muscular frame. With a parting look from his near-to-green eyes, he headed toward the shower. *We'll talk when he's ready*, Scott decided.

Within moments Braxton heard the crackling attempt at song, as Scott's raspy voice was barely disguised by the rush of cascading water. He held back a chuckle when the toneless voice grew louder in competition with the shower.

Turning his attention back to the designs, Braxton tried in vain to focus his attention on the plans in front of him. His mind kept wandering back to Tempest. Something just didn't make sense, but he couldn't put his finger on it. Maybe she just needed more time to get used to seeing him after so long and so suddenly before she could begin to trust him again. With enough persistence and gentle patience on his part, they could settle what lay between them. He was sure of it. It was just her stubborn pride that stood in the way. What other possible explanation could there be? There was no way that he was going to believe that she had stopped loving him, just as he had not stopped loving her. He knew her too well. Tempest ran from the things that threatened her stability. And his reappearance was certainly a threat to that stability.

At that point Scott emerged from the shower. His dark brown hair was almost black as it lay plastered to his skull. Large wet feet made a distinct outline on the heavy carpet. Scott, of course, took no notice. The only thing Scott had ever been conscientious about, for as long as Braxton had known him, was his work. On that score Braxton would lay his firm on the line in defense of his dearest friend. Watching him now brought back a rush of boyhood memories, and Braxton realized that a night out with Scott might be just the medicine he needed.

"You know what, buddy? I've changed my mind. I think I'll join you. Exploring the big city is just what we need."

"I knew you'd come around to my way of thinking," Scott said with a mischievous grin. "Let me throw on some clothes and I'll be ready in about a half hour." He went through the door to the adjoining bedroom, feeling that he had accomplished his mission. Hopefully Braxton would snap out of it and talk with him, if not tonight then sometime soon. But until then Scott promised himself that he'd be in Braxton's corner when he needed him.

Maybe the evening won't be so bad after all, Braxton thought, regaining some of his old spunk, as he took his turn in the steaming shower. *Not so bad at all.*

Tempest was glad that she'd driven to work. At least she wouldn't have to compete with the rush of employees fighting for cabs. After hours of shopping for her finicky clients, she was weighted down with sample fabric and wall coverings.

Slipping behind the wheel of her silver Mercedes Benz convertible, she tossed her packages on the backseat, gunned the engine, and slid easily into the flow of rush-hour traffic.

Wanting to catch the last rays of dying sunshine and feel the still balmy spring air rush against her, she depressed the button that rolled back the hood of her car. Flipping on her favorite jazz station, she hummed along, her mood lightened for the first time in days. Checking the digital clock, she realized that she still had two hours to relax before her dinner engagement with David.

Then on impulse Tempest decided to take a quick trip to see her grandmother. It had been weeks since she'd visited her. The time she'd spent in the past months preparing for the showing in South America had left little time for the woman who raised her. A nagging feeling of guilt assailed her. Although Tempest made it a point to visit her often, sometimes there just weren't enough hours in a day, and she worried about her constantly. Her grandmother had suffered two heart attacks in as many years, but still she refused to let Tempest pay for a housekeeper to look after her and do the heavier work around her home. But she made a silent pledge to herself to be more diligent. She was sure she couldn't bear it if something were to happen to her grandmother. The short visit would do them both good. Besides, she needed to talk with her grandmother.

Swinging the car onto Sixth Avenue, she headed toward Central Park. If she could catch all of the green lights, she could reach Eighty-sixth Street in no time.

Fifteen minutes later she pulled up in front of her grandmother's townhouse. Tempest felt a pull of pride at having been able to provide this small luxury for her grandmother. Although she felt she owed her so much more, this token of her thanks was the least she could do.

Running up the short flight of steps, she pressed on the soundless chimes. Moments later the stout Ella Dailey appeared at the glass doors. The expression of surprise and happiness on her face was well worth the detour, Tempest thought, completely satisfied with her last-minute decision.

"Baby girl, what are you doing here?" Ella swung open the door and grabbed her granddaughter in a bear hug.

"I thought I'd surprise you, Gram," Tempest grinned, returning the warm welcome.

"Well, you sure did. Come on in here, girl." Wrapping a heavy arm around Tempest, she ushered her into the front room.

The entire house was totally of Ella's homespun design. She'd refused years ago to let Tempest design the townhouse for her. She'd said, "Your tastes are far too flashy for my simple ways. There's no way these hips could slide into those tiny modern chairs you'd have me sit in." So Tempest had let her have her way. Admittedly Ella had done a splendid job. The warm earth tones mixed with yellows and floral prints gave each of the rooms a country atmosphere.

Taking her favorite seat next to the window, Ella pressed Tempest for details of her hectic life.

"So tell me, baby girl, how is everything? You look tired. Have you been getting enough rest?" she queried, with her motherly concern. Her dark eyes peered at her granddaughter through thick bifocals. "It's not like you to do things on the spur of the moment. Are you sure nothing's wrong?"

"You don't miss a trick, do you, Gram?"

"Not when it comes to you. So tell me. What is it?"

Tempest began unwinding the events of the past two days. Ten minutes later she sat facing her grandmother, patiently waiting for the words that she hoped would comfort her.

"I just don't know what to do, Gram. I still love him, but I'm so afraid that he'll hurt me again."

"Now you listen to me," began Ella, ready to stand on her pulpit. "That man walked out on you once before, and look where it got you. What makes you think he won't do it again? And what about Kai? You have to think about her, too. If you want to ruin your own life, that's one thing, but I'm not going to stand idly by and let that man hurt my great-granddaughter. What do you think it would do to that child if he became a part of her life and then left?"

"But maybe if I told him—"

"Told him?" Ella felt panic grip her insides. She pushed herself up from her seat and paced the floor, twisting and untwisting her hands as she walked. "What could you possibly be thinkin'? You want to turn your whole world upside down for some man who wouldn't give you the time of day when you needed him? And what about your husband, or did you forget him? You plannin' on just walkin' out on him after all he done for you?"

Tempest watched, frozen and perplexed, at the transformation that had taken place. Ella's eyes literally blazed with fury, as she punctuated each word with exaggerated flailing of her arms.

This wasn't what she expected. Her grandmother's reaction seemed totally disproportionate to the situation. But maybe she was wrong for even bringing it up with her grandmother, knowing full well the bond that existed between Ella and Kai, and her devout loyalty to David. She had always trusted Ella's judgment in the past, but for the first time she had a feeling of doubt. Yet she understood her concern.

"Gram, please calm down." Tempest stood next to her and braced her shoulders, looking her straight in the eye. "You're right," she admitted half-heartedly. She felt a shudder of relief race through Ella's body. "Some things are better left alone."

Ella took a deep breath and searched Tempest's eyes for any sign of doubt in her words.

"It's best, baby girl—believe me." She pulled Tempest into the folds of her arms and placed a kiss on her cheek. "Have I ever steered you wrong?"

"No, Gram," Tempest said with the hint of a smile, "Never. Listen," she said, wanting to change the subject and escape the strained atmosphere. "I've got to get home and get ready. I have a dinner date with David."

"David—" Ella shook her head. "I never could understand why you can't just forget Braxton. David is such a good man. He's the perfect husband and father. Hundreds of women would love to be in your shoes."

Tempest felt another lecture coming. "Gram, let's not get into that again."

"You have to try harder. Marriage is supposed to be forever." She walked beside Tempest to the door.

Turning to wrap her grandmother in a final hug, Tempest bid her farewell, choosing not to make any further comment on her grandmother's staunch convictions. "Don't forget to take your medicine, and I'll see you on the weekend." She blew her grandmother a kiss and descended the stairs.

"Bring Kai, or don't come," Ella called to the departing figure.

Tempest flashed a quick smile in response and sped away.

Ella stood on the steps of her townhouse. Her heart pounded heavily in her chest. What had she done? All the years of lies and indiscretions were coming back to haunt her. She'd done what she did out of love and a promise to her daughter that she'd do everything in her power to see that Tempest had a good, secure life. But if Tempest ever found out the whole truth, she'd never forgive her for what she had done. Suddenly she grabbed her chest as a searing pain ripped through her. The last thing she remembered before blackness overtook her was that, for the first time in her life, she doubted her judgment—and that it was too late to make amends.

With only an hour left before the limousine was due to arrive, Tempest spent some time with Kai, putting her to bed, and then quickly preparing for her engagement. Freshly showered, she dusted her body in her favorite scent and pulled on a white, lightweight wool dress with gold embroidery down the front. She made the final touches to her hair and makeup. Off-white sling-back shoes and matching purse set off the outfit to perfection. As she took a final glimpse in the mirror, the doorbell rang and she dashed for the elevator. David abhorred lateness, and she certainly wasn't in the mood for one of his lectures about etiquette. Having listened to her grandmother's well-meant words of wisdom was enough for one day.

For the first time in hours, Tempest was finally able to relax. The motion of the car was soothing. Soft music floated to her ears from the hidden stereo speakers, and she let her body unwind. This was a far cry from the last time she rode in this very same car, she thought ruefully, while she wondered what David's plan of attack would be tonight.

✕

Moments later she was swiftly escorted to her table at Jezebel's. The decor had changed once again from the last time she was there, she noted as she glided past the white linen topped tables and wicker lounging chairs. The room was adorned with tropical plants.

82

The Bird of Paradise was the focal point. One of these plants stood majestically on each of the tables. Lilies of the Valley floated in huge glass vases on top of the grand piano, while the pianist played to the enthusiastic crowd. Jezebel's was renowned for its southern cuisine, and patrons from all walks of life crowded the intimate dining room to capacity every night.

Easing by a Tiffany-shaded lamp, she caught a quick glimpse of Christine, one of New York's hottest models, accompanied by a gorgeous man, who, if he wasn't, should have been in the movies.

David had chosen her favorite table. From the very first time that they had dined there together she'd fallen in love with the white, wooden bench swing in the rear of the restaurant. He made a point of selecting that table each time they'd come thereafter. Maybe tonight wouldn't be so bad after all, she thought as she slid into the swing, giving David a warm smile.

"You look stunning as always. I hope you're hungry. I took the liberty of ordering your favorite."

"How thoughtful of you, David," she said, barely containing a smile. He always had to be a step ahead, or he wasn't happy, she thought.

"I tried your office earlier. I was told that you'd gone *shopping.*" His tone clearly indicated how frivolous he thought that aspect of her job was.

"As I told you yesterday, I *do* have other clients who need my services as well. We are working on the renovation of an estate on Long Island."

"I hardly consider shopping for fabric using your extraordinary talent to the fullest. You could utilize yourself so much better if you would reconsider this housing complex—"

Tempest held up her hand to forestall any further discussion on the subject.

"I thought I made myself clear. I cannot take on this project. After careful consideration of the time and effort that would be necessary, there is no way that I could handle it. But if you would be willing to consider letting Bridgette be in charge of the interior work, I'm sure that something could be worked out."

David's whole demeanor stiffened. That was not what he had in mind at all. "We've discussed this before. Bridgette is not you. She's good, don't get me wrong. Just not good enough. If you cannot see to this job personally, then I have no other choice but to find someone or some other firm equally capable of handling it. On that note the subject is closed," he stated with finality, taking a quick sip of his wine.

Tempest started to protest, when her eye caught a flash in the mirrored pillars. Standing near the piano waiting to be seated were Scott Hamilton and Braxton. Her stomach did a somersault, as she took a quick gulp of wine. *How much worse can my luck get?* Her panic rose as she watched the handsome duo edge closer. Within moments they would see her, and there was only one ready exit—the one they had just entered. She certainly could not spend the balance of the evening in the ladies' room, she thought miserably. She'd just have to make the best of it. If there was any justice in the world, maybe they wouldn't see her.

As fate would have it, David, too, saw them enter, and stood up to wave them toward his and Tempest's table. Maybe there would be a freak earthquake, she prayed, as they neared the table.

"Braxton, please join us. I take it this is your partner, Mr. Hamilton." David extended a hand to Scott. "It's a pleasure to meet you." Making a motion to the waiter to bring two chairs, David resumed his seat.

Tempest tried to keep her gaze averted from Braxton, but she was continually drawn to the exquisitely dressed man. He still wore linen, but this time it was a pale blue suit. The single-breasted jacket and pleated pants gave him a casual air, with a touch of class. A white cotton, collarless shirt offset the outfit.

Scott, on the other hand, was immaculate in an Italian business suit of dark blue, a perfect compliment to his light tones. How long had it been since she'd seen Scott? He'd certainly changed his mode of dress since graduate school, she thought, amused.

"Mr. Hamilton, let me introduce my wife. Tempest, Scott Hamilton, Mr. Thorne's partner."

Scott bent his head to plant a kiss on Tempest's hand. "It's a pleasure to meet you. B.J. here has told me a lot about you."

"Really?" David interjected before Tempest could respond.

"Good things, I hope," she added quickly.

"Definitely," Scott quipped with a rakish smile.

David watched the exchange in silence as his suspicions and anger mounted.

"Actually," Braxton jumped in, seeing the pained look on Tempest's face, "our table is ready. Scott and I have a lot of catching up to do about the business back home. We wouldn't want to bore you with shop talk tonight. So if you'll excuse us," he said, rising from his seat and nudging his friend.

Over his shoulder he added, "I'll have those preliminary sketches to you by the end of next week, Mr. Lang, as soon as I see the land."

"I'll be making other arrangements to have you escorted out there. Call my office. My secretary will give you the information."

"Sure thing." The two men were shown to their table, separated from Tempest's by only one other couple.

The balance of the evening was endless. When dinner arrived, Tempest didn't remember eating anything, as she spent most of her time struggling to avoid the furtive glances that were shot her way from Braxton. The honeyed yams and normally mouthwatering batter-dipped chicken with mixed vegetables all tasted like cardboard. Somehow she managed to hold up her end of the stilted conversation and gave a silent sigh of relief when the waiter cleared the table, and David requested the check.

Braxton and Scott were still seated when Tempest and David rose to leave. They could not avoid passing by them on the way out, unless they walked completely around the dining room. Guided by David's sure hand on her elbow, they stopped at their table.

"Mr. Hamilton, it was good meeting you. I look forward to the three of us working together," he said, pointedly excluding Tempest.

Braxton and Scott rose from their seats and the group said their good-byes. Tempest felt a moment of relief as they exited the restaurant. However, as she stepped into the chauffeur-driven limousine, she had the sinking feeling that the worst was yet to come.

Chapter Six

The short car ride home was a nightmare. Tempest chattered mindlessly about every inconsequential event that she could think of in an effort to break the tension that had deposited itself between her and David since the awkward meeting at the restaurant.

He sat next to her in stony silence, intermittently punctuating the air with nods and grunts at all of the appropriate places. Yet she knew that David neither heard nor cared about anything she was saying. She watched his face as she continued to babble about the trouble she was having with her client, Mrs. Washington, and how grown up Kai had gotten while she was away. But he remained unaffected by her words. The look behind his eyes was one to which she'd become accustomed. A steely calm pervaded his smooth features, in sharp contrast to the fury that lay beneath.

It was the same look he had each and every time he set out to rid himself of an obstacle. Other times she would have ignored it. This time was different, vaguer, more chilling. As sure as she was that there were stars in the heavens, she was sure she was that obstacle.

The limo glided to a halt in front of their loft. David jumped out and was en route to the door before the chauffeur rounded the car. The startled driver helped Tempest out of the car and escorted her to the elevator.

David's rigid back remained turned as Tempest approached. She stood apart from him, wary of the invisible barrier he had constructed around himself.

If only he would yell, scream, anything, she thought, just confront her with what he was feeling. But she knew that he wouldn't. David was too controlled for that. Exhibiting emotion was something he rarely did.

To their surprise, the lights were blazing when they entered the apartment. Clara rushed to meet them at the door, tears streaming down her face.

Panic assaulted Tempest. She felt every fiber of her being go cold within her.

"Is it Kai?" Tempest grabbed the hysterical Clara.

Clara shook her head and between gulps

explained that she'd only moments ago received a call from Mt. Sinai hospital, informing her that Tempest's grandmother had suffered a massive heart attack. She'd been found in her doorway by a neighbor and rushed to the hospital.

"Oh, God," Tempest moaned. "I've got to see her." She turned imploringly to David, who pulled her into his arms.

"Call my driver, Clara. Tell him to get here immediately," he commanded. "And bring my wife a glass of brandy."

His authoritative manner seemed to snap Clara out of her frantic state as she quickly followed his instructions. He put Tempest at arm's length, tilting up her chin to meet his eyes, his words willing her to come to grips with what lay ahead.

"Now you listen to me. You cannot fall apart. You won't be doing yourself or Ella any good. I know you're thinking the worst, but we can't be sure of anything until we speak with the doctors."

Clara returned with the glass of brandy.

"Here, drink this. You'll feel better." Then to Clara, "Did you get my driver?"

"He'll be here in five minutes."

"Thank you. Why don't you go and try to get some sleep. We'll phone you if there is a need."

"Yes, Mr. Lang." Clara patted Tempest's hand, and the look in her pain-filled eyes conveyed more than any words of sympathy could express.

When they arrived at the hospital, they were quickly escorted to the office of Dr. James, the cardio-vascular specialist who was handling the case.

"I'm glad you both arrived so quickly. Please sit down and let me explain Mrs. Dailey's condition." He opened the chart that lay on his desk.

"Will she be all right?" Tempest broke in, unable to withstand another moment of not knowing.

David gripped her hand and pulled her into a seat. "Let the doctor speak." Tempest took a deep breath and waited.

Dr. James measured his words. "Your grand-mother has sustained a massive heart attack. The lack of blood flow and the resulting shock to the body have caused her to slip into a coma."

Tempest bit down on her lip, momentarily clos-ing her eyes against the onslaught of his words. But she said nothing.

"How long will she be in this coma, and what is the extent of the damage to her heart?" asked David.

"We can't answer that now. At the moment we have her on life support to help her breathe. The next seventy-two hours will tell."

Tempest asked the question that weighted down her soul. "Is my grandmother going to die?" She want-ed to snatch back the words, but she had to know. She faced the doctor eye-to-eye.

"We're doing everything we can."

"Then you're going to have to do more," David stated simply and rose from his seat once again assuming a commanding air. "Money is no object. I want a round-the-clock nurse, and I'll have the best specialists in the country here in the morning."

"Well, I think we're quite capable of—"

"I'm sure that you are. However, those are *my* instructions, and that's what will be done."

Gordon James always did have a strong distaste for the wealthy elite. No matter how hard you tried, they felt that their money could buy better. Yet his heart went out to this pompous man's wife, who he could plainly see was using her last bit of reserve to hold herself together. He admired that, and applauded the resiliency that it no doubt took to live with such a man—running for political office or not.

Dr. James snapped the chart shut and responded calmly. "If that's what you want, Mr. Lang."

"That's what we want, doctor."

Gordon James seriously doubted that but chose not to let a comment slip.

"Can we see her now, doctor?" Her voice sounded stronger than she appeared.

"Yes, but only for a few minutes. I'll take you to her room."

"You two go on. I'll meet you over there. I have some calls to make."

※

The muted bleeps of the monitor and the ghostly hissing of the respirator reverberating off the stark walls only added to the heavy layer of guilt that rested on Tempest's shoulders. As she sat, still as a statue in her vigil, the doctor's words to her crept back into her consciousness. "This attack could have been brought on only by severe stress and anxiety—" A knot of guilt twisted in her stomach.

Holding her grandmother's cold, parched hand in her own, she prayed. She prayed for this woman who was the only mother she had ever known, who gave of herself and sacrificed so that she could have the best that life had to offer.

Her heart ached in a way that she never imagined it could, as she helplessly watched the still form beneath the sterile white sheets. What had she done? She should have known better. She was the reason that her Gram lay there. If she could just be given a second chance, she'd make it up to her, she swore in silent promise. She would do anything, give anything, to have Ella well again.

※

She didn't hear him enter or know that he had stood for many moments watching her. She turned with a start at the sound of his voice.

"There's nothing more you can do here, Mrs. Lang," Dr. James said gently. "I saw your husband in the hallway, and it appears that he has assembled all of the players." He gave her a lopsided smile.

Tempest wearily rose from her watch, giving the hand in hers a parting kiss. "You have to excuse my husband," she said softly. "He tends to be rather over-bearing at times, but he means well."

"They generally do." He gave her the full bene-fit of his smile, and for the first time he saw the begin-nings of a smile in return.

"I'll walk you to the elevator."

As they walked together down the long corridor, David's impassive figure loomed ahead. Gordon felt his protective instincts rush to the surface.

"Are you going to be all right? Do you think you'll need something to help you sleep?"

"That's not what you mean at all, is it?" Her in-tuitiveness both startled and embarrassed him. He did-n't realize he was so transparent. It was just that he could not visualize this lovely woman consciously in the arms of such a cold man.

"I didn't mean anything. It's just that—"

"It's all right, doctor." She managed a small ten-tative smile. "I'll be just fine. Thank you for every-thing." Taking a deep, cleansing breath, she moved for-ward with quiet dignity.

He stood there for many moments after the ele-vator doors had shut behind them, and somehow he knew that she would be all right.

><><

Tempest was somewhat disappointed but genuinely relieved that David had opted to spend the night in the guest room. It would have been more than she could handle if he had tried to console her. Although that was highly unlikely, she reminded herself, as the steaming shower raced down and massaged her weary body. It had been months since she and David had truly been man and wife. Yet now even with all that she had on her mind, as she trailed the creamy soap over her limbs, the desire for the fiery touch of a man to wipe away the pain and loneliness leaped within her with such force that an unstoppable moan escaped her lips.

She closed her eyes against the intensity of her feelings while invisible hands caressed her in places that she had forgotten, awakening sensations that were dormant. Fantasy bluffed her vision and Braxton stood before her, peeling away the hurt and loneliness.

She allowed her body to succumb to the powers of her mind, if only for a moment. But as the cascading waters were drawn back into their reservoir, so were her illusions drawn back into the recesses of her heart. She so needed someone to truly love and to love her back. But she had her work and she had Kai, and at times like last night she had David, she reminded herself. Those things would have to suffice.

✳✳

The apartment was quiet when she emerged from her room. David had apparently left for his office, and Clara had seen Kai off to school while she slept. She found Clara sitting at the kitchen table, absently folding and unfolding towels.

"Morning, Clara. Were you able to get any sleep?"

"Not much. But I didn't expect that I would."

"I guess David told you what the doctor said."

Clara sniffed back impending tears and only nodded in response.

"Well, I'm going to the hospital before I go in to the office. Are you going before Kai gets in?"

"I'm gonna stop by the church first. But I'll be there, don't you worry none."

Tempest reached over and hugged Clara long and hard. The two women transferred and drew strength from each other, then parted without further words—each knowing what was in the other's heart.

✳✳

Unable to sleep, David had arrived at his office before dawn. There were plans to be made and events to be put into motion. Now with the added distraction of Ella's illness looming over Tempest, it would make his job a bit more difficult. But that was not what concerned him. He had been lax, which was a trait foreign to him.

He stared at the courier-delivered report in front of him and seethed. He should have done his homework on Braxton Thorne long before now. Only this morning he had learned that there was a prior relationship between Thorne and his wife, confirming his suspicions. But there was more, and Marty Jackson had uncovered that as well.

Jackson was the best private investigator in the business. If there was anything to be found, Jackson would find it. He was expected back later that afternoon, and David was sure he would have something that he could use to his advantage. He smiled a secret smile and momentarily felt content.

ATLANTA

Long red fingernails tapped out a nervous rhythm against the highly polished, black lacquer desk. The sound echoed across the expanse of the inner sanctuary, amplifying the anxiety that reigned in her veins. A tremulous hand sought the key that unlocked the bottom drawer and withdrew a sterling silver flask. The golden liquid was warm as it crept slowly down her throat, thawing her insides, calming her pounding heart. *Why is this man coming to see me? What does he know?*

The thought that she might have been found out caused fresh panic to flow. But she couldn't risk taking another drink. She had to be alert. There was no room for error.

The sudden buzz of her intercom caused her to jump. She quickly replaced the flask and locked the drawer. Taking a deep breath, she answered.

"Mr. Jackson is here to see you."

"Send him right in, Cynthia."

She stood up and smoothed her red silk dress and stepped toward the door, just as Marty Jackson entered.

"Mr. Jackson," she said, putting on all of her southern charm. "Do come in."

Without looking closely, she appeared beautiful, flawless. But on closer scrutiny, he could detect the signs of deterioration: eyes that remained slightly glazed, full lips that turned just a bit down at the corners, a hard edge to a once melodious voice. The high yellow complexion held a flush that wouldn't go away—and always the telltale tremor of the hands. He had seen the signs too many times in the past to miss them. *Alcohol will do it every time,* he mused. "May I sit down?"

"Why don't we sit on the couch where we'll be more comfortable?" she crooned, patting the seat next to her.

Marty held back a chuckle that bubbled in his throat. *She is a real number.*

"I'll get straight to the point. I already know that you're in a lot of debt."

"I beg your—"

"Look, let's not play games. This is a nice little gig you have here, runnin' this museum. But it don't pay you nearly what you need to cover your, uh, expenses."

"I think you'd better leave, Mr. Jackson." She tilted her chin in defiance and attempted to stand.

He grabbed her wrist. "I think you'd better listen. I have a proposition for you."

Twenty minutes later the faint light of freedom peaked at the end of a long, dark tunnel. There was finally a way out. The money that she had been offered could solve all of her problems. He was right. Being curator of Atlanta's finest museum in no way met her needs. So she'd had to find other resources to supplement her income.

It had been so easy at first. She simply sold museum merchandise on the black market and then bought back the same pieces. Lately the cost of buying back the objects had skyrocketed, and she couldn't meet the prices. What was more frightening was the quarterly inventory that was coming up in less than two months. Everything had to be accounted for. Now that was no longer an impossibility. One hundred thousand dollars would cure all of her ills.

"I think we have a deal, Mr. Jackson."

"I was sure that we would. The rest is up to you.

Your plane ticket will be waiting at the airport. You'll be contacted as to when."

"It will be a pleasure to see my old adversary again," she cooed in a malevolent voice.

He extended a calloused hand. "It's been a pleasure doing business with you, Mrs. Thorne."

"The pleasure," she drawled, "will be all mine."

Chapter Seven

The visit to the hospital had left Tempest with an inkling of hope. As David had promised, two heart specialists and a neurologist had been flown in from California, and the private-duty nurse sat diligently at her post.

Ella's vital signs were weak but steady, and the doctor felt that she might be able to breathe on her own in several days.

There had been no brain damage, according to the CAT scan, but a by-pass operation was definitely necessary. Even though she was still in a coma, at least the prognosis was good, Tempest reminded herself, as she stepped off of the elevator and headed toward her office.

When she entered, Bridgette was there to meet her. Her expression was filled with sympathy and something more.

"Clara called this morning and told me," she said gently. "I'm so sorry. How is she?"

Tempest managed a weak smile and sighed out a response, unable to meet Bridgette's eyes.

"The doctors say she's doing better, but they will have to operate this time, when she's stronger."

"She's going to be fine," Bridgette assured. "Ella's a tough old cookie." Bridgette saw the anguish that rimmed Tempest's eyes and dreaded what she must tell her.

"Listen, hon," she began slowly, "I know your whole world is upside down right now, and I hate to bombard you with this, but we have a serious problem." Tempest braced herself. What else could possibly go wrong?

"Mrs. Washington called this morning. She's canceled her contract."

"What?"

"She said she no longer needed our services— and that she would have her lawyer contact us."

Shock yielded quickly to rage. "She can't do that!"

"She seems to think that she can."

"Did she at least give you a reason?"

"When I asked her, she got very flustered and refused to discuss it."

Unconsciously Tempest's brow furrowed, her eyes gazed off into the distance. "Fine," she replied finally. "We'll just concentrate our efforts on our other projects, that's all."

Bridgette took a deep breath. "That's not all."

Tempest shot her an apprehensive look.

"The project that I've been working on—" she hesitated, "well, the Monroes also decided they couldn't use our services any longer."

Stunned, Tempest sank down into her chair like a deflated balloon. Her mind whirled with bewilderment. For several moments she sat perfectly still, eyes unblinking as though in a trance as she absorbed the magnitude of their situation. Those were their two biggest accounts. Together they were worth millions. The company's entire quarterly budget hinged on those two projects. This was too coincidental, too unprovoked. She'd never lost a client in all of the years she'd been in business. Why now?

Her pride concealed her inner turmoil and against all of her instincts, she knew what she must do for the good of her company. Her back was firmly against the wall. Keeping all expression from her voice, she spoke.

"It looks as though we have no other alternative than to take the project in Jersey."

Bridgette saw in Tempest's eyes what it cost her to say those words and admired her all the more. "I know how difficult it will be for you, but we have to think of this in the long term."

Tempest nodded her assent. She and survival

were longtime friends. She'd endured more than this in the past, and she would handle this new crisis as well.

With a clear look of determination and a smile of firm resolve, she pulled the sketches out of the cabinet, instructed Bridgette to contact David, and then got down to the business at hand, momentarily snuffing the embers of her suspicions.

❧❦❧

"I'm glad to hear that, Bridgette. What made her change her mind? I know how stubborn my wife can be."

"I'd prefer you discuss that with Tempest. However, if tomorrow is still good, she'll arrange to meet Mr. Thorne out at the site."

"Both he and Mr. Hamilton are with me right now. I'm sure that it won't be a problem. Tell Tempest I'll speak with her later today."

David gently replaced the receiver. Looking up he gave them the benefit of his most benevolent smile, triumph ringing in his voice.

"Well, gentlemen, it appears that my wife has had a change of heart. She's willing to work on the project after all. She'll meet you out there tomorrow. I guess she finally realized how important her participation in this is for me, both politically and emotionally." He put his hand to his heart in blatant affectation.

Braxton cringed inside at the display of feigned

emotion.

"Then, too," David continued unperturbed, "with her grandmother's sudden heart attack, the busier she is, the better."

Braxton felt a quick pull in his gut. Tempest's grandmother meant the world to her. She was probably devastated. And this obtuse man didn't seem to care one way or the other.

"I'm sorry to hear that, Mr. Lang," Braxton said, using all of his self-control to hide his contempt.

David strolled toward the windows, peering out onto the street below, and shrugged matter-of-factly. "Please don't concern yourself. I've already seen to it that the best specialists are working on her. I'm sure she'll be fine," he added absently.

"I'm sure," Braxton replied with mild sarcasm.

"I think we'd better be going," Scott jumped in, accurately assessing Braxton's darkening mood. Scott gave him a nudge, and the two men rose to leave.

"I'll have the contracts brought over to your hotel. All I'll need is your signatures, and we can get started."

David extended his hand to Braxton and Scott and escorted them to the door.

David stood momentarily in the center of his office, viewing his world. Everything was going according to plan. The housing complex would be on schedule, which would surely clinch his election bid. Tempest was in line, and Jackson had come up with the finishing touch. His mouth pulled into a wry grin. Money *could* buy you everything, and he had no intention of ever being poor, unnoticed, or unimportant again. He'd proven them all wrong: his mother, his teachers, and those filthy, vulgar children in the old neighborhood. He gave a shiver of vivid recollection but quickly shook away the disturbing vision. Returning to his desk, he pressed the intercom for his secretary.

"Yes, Mr. Lang?"

"Has my lawyer reviewed those contracts?"

"Mr. Lang. Everything is ready."

"Bring them in please, and call Joseph Ackerman. Put him right through when you reach him." David reclined in his chair and smiled a satisfied smile.

✄

"There's something not quite right about this whole deal, B.J." Scott said, as he maneuvered their rented midnight blue Porsche into the flow of afternoon traffic. "I think we need to pull out."

"We can't do that," Braxton stated simply.

"Of course we can. We haven't signed anything yet."

"Listen, I know Lang isn't the most likeable person in the world, but he's high powered. He has connections. This job could be our entree into many others. We need this. I need this. The money we'll receive will set the company straight and could mean my freedom. I'll finally be able to offer Jasmine a settlement that she'll agree with."

"You know I'm with you all the way," Scott conceded. "I just hope that it's worth it. That Lang gives me a real uneasy feeling."

Braxton stared pensively out the window, just as they passed a billboard heralding David Lang as the next congressman of New York. Braxton gave an involuntary shudder at the thought.

Tempest sat at Kai's bedside and in gentle tones explained to her that her great-grandmother was in the hospital. After answering countless questions and assuring her that Ella would be with them again soon, she waited until Kai was soundly asleep before she left her side.

She entered the living room just as David came in, and something inside of her went cold. All of her misgivings resurfaced and etched themselves on her face. She stood stock still with both hands on her hips as she faced him.

"Is something wrong?" He offhandedly tossed his briefcase onto the chair. "You look as though you're ready to do battle."

"Cut the crap, David. Why did you do it?"

"I certainly don't know what you're talking about." He turned away as if to dismiss her.

"You know perfectly well what I'm talking about." She hurled the words at him like stones. "Somehow you managed to pull two of my biggest accounts out from under me."

He retained his complacency as he turned back to face her, but there was a subtle hardening of his eyes.

"You couldn't honestly believe that I would do something like that. This is the first I'm hearing of it." Indignation and hurt tinged his voice. He flung his overcoat onto the chair. "Why would you think such a thing? Do you believe I'm that much of a monster?"

Her resolve faltered. Maybe he didn't know anything about it and she was just drawing too many conclusions.

"It's probably some kind of bizarre coincidence. Did that ever occur to you before you unjustly accused me? I helped you get some of your biggest clients. Remember?"

Deep inside she didn't want to believe that he would stoop to sabotaging his own wife. She must be wrong.

"I'm sorry, David." She took a tentative step toward him and ran a hand through her hair. "It's just that with so much going on in my life right now I guess I'm not thinking clearly. Then to lose those two accounts when I knew that you wanted me on this project, I guess I just—"

"Granted, I did and still do want you to work on this with me but not at the expense of your company. I would never do anything like that—and surely nothing to hurt you. I thought you knew that by now." He reached out to her, and she stepped into his arms. She searched his eyes.

"It's all right," he said in soothing tones, as he stroked her hair. "I know you're going through hell right now, but I'm here for you. Don't forget that."

He tilted her face up to his, his mouth descending onto hers, drawing her closer against him.

She gave in to the demands of her body, so wanting the closeness of someone. And then without warning he pulled away.

"Ask Clara if she'll pack a bag for me, will you? I have to go out of town again. My campaign manager has arranged for some appearances upstate and two news conferences. My plane leaves in an hour." She stared, speechless.

"I know this is a bad time for you, but duty calls. I'll be home by the weekend." He planted a cool kiss on her cheek, and ran his hand down her hip pulling her snugly against him. "Next time," he breathed in her ear, "I'll take you and Kai with me. How's that?"

But before she could gather her senses to respond, he had gone off in the direction of Kai's room. She turned on her heel and went to seek out Clara.

The driver slid into an available space in front of the departure terminal and rounded the car to remove the bags from the trunk.

The backseat passenger removed a narrow mani-la envelope from the breast pocket of his Perry Ellis suit and handed it to the passenger beside him.

"For your troubles. You'll find the usual amount and a little bonus."

"My pleasure."

"I have one more job for you." He removed two overstuffed envelopes from his briefcase. "First thing tomorrow morning, I want you to deliver these. The addresses are on the front."

"Sure thing."

"And, Jackson, don't be late. Mrs. Washington and Mr. and Mrs. Monroe are expecting these before noon."

"Have I ever let you down, Mr. Lang?"

David gave a look of pained tolerance, stepped from the car and was quickly swallowed up in the surge of travelers.

Marty Jackson stole a furtive glance into the en-velopes and let out a silent whistle of disbelief. Both were filled to near bursting with crisp one-hundred-dol-lar bills. There had to easily be one hundred and fifty thousand dollars in each, he calculated.

He wondered momentarily what "good deed" these folks had done to make his benefactor so gener-ous.

Chapter Eight

BLOOMFIELD, NEW JERSEY

Every nerve in her body was pulled to the breaking point. It took all of her concentration to keep her eyes on the road. Maneuvering around the winding turns, she experienced a gamut of turbulent emotions. All of her loneliness, pain, confusion, and wanting welded together in one surge of yearning—for Braxton. The thought of being alone with him set her pulse racing.

She knew that what she was feeling was wrong. She was a married woman, and Braxton had hurt her in a way that no other man had or could. But she couldn't deny the irresistible pull that she still felt for him.

It was obvious that fate was playing a major role in her life. How else could one explain him being repeatedly thrown in her path? It must be for a reason, mustn't it?

No! She must get a handle on her emotions. Here she was envisioning an affair with him when there were still so many things unresolved between them, and the stability of her family to consider. Her mind reeled in confusion.

Within minutes she would arrive at the site, and he would be there. They would be there—together. What was she going to do? How was she ever going to survive this? Her heart raced in time with the speeding auto, which was rapidly closing the distance between them.

✠

Braxton and Scott had just completed their survey of the grounds as Tempest's car pulled up in front of the cluster of buildings.

Braxton's pulse quickened, and he took an involuntary step toward her car. Scott grabbed his wrist.

"Whoa! Take it easy, man. One step at a time. Remember?"

Braxton took a pausing breath and gave a half-hearted smile. "That's going to be damn hard when every time I see her all I can think about is taking her in my arms and never letting go."

"Well, try," Scott teased.

At that point Tempest stepped from her car. She felt that at any moment her knees would give out and she'd collapse in an embarrassed heap. *He is so beautiful*, she thought as his form drew closer with her every step. It took all she had not to run into his arms, forgetting all else except the two of them together. That was ridiculous of course. She must keep her mind on business—*too much to lose*, she recited to herself, *too much to lose—*

She was casually dressed, he noted with pleasure, looking so much like he remembered her in college. Her shoulder-length hair was pulled back into a ponytail. Her faded jeans accentuated her slender hips and endlessly long legs. She wore an oversized, eggshell white sweater and a pair of blue and white *Nike* sneakers. She looked beautiful, he concluded, his heart thumping wildly with her every approaching footfall.

"Good morning, gentlemen." Did her voice go up two octaves, or was it her imagination? She reached up on tiptoe and planted a light kiss on Scott's cheek. "It's good to see you again. I'm sorry about the other night. I didn't mean to put you on the spot, but I appreciated your discretion."

Scott smiled a smile of understanding that can be found only between close friends.

She turned to Braxton and gave him a curt nod, not daring to speak lest her voice give her away.

Braxton merely nodded in return. *She's just as nervous as I am.*

There was an awkward moment of silence between them until Scott broke the ice.

"Well, folks, let's get to work," he said a bit too enthusiastically. But both Tempest and Braxton breathed a silent sigh of relief. "We've set up a make-shift office down in the last building at the edge of the hill," he added with a nod of his head in that direction.

The trio marched off in silence in the direction of the office, the balmy spring air electrified with the bottled-up emotions barely held in abeyance.

Initially Braxton and Tempest said little to each other. Thankfully Scott did most of the talking. They made concerted efforts to maintain a safe distance between them, frightened of what the slightest touch might generate. But several hours later, with the subtle aid of Scott and mountains of work behind them, the three were laughing and joking like old times, anxiety all but forgotten.

"But remember the homecoming picnic and the freak thunderstorm?" Scott asked. "Ms. Homecoming Queen was all dolled up in her Sunday best and wound up looking like a wet rag."

Braxton's deep basso laugh echoed throughout the cavernous building, running like a maestro's fingers on a grand piano up Tempest's spine.

"And everybody paired off and ran for cover. Remember?" Scott added, slapping his thigh and shaking his head at the vision.

As if on cue, Tempest and Braxton looked at each other and the air stood still. The memory was so powerful it took them both by surprise.

Our first time together, she said with her eyes. *How could I ever forget?*

I lost myself to you that day, he said in silent response. *For then and always.*

Scott instantly felt locked out, as the two shared a look and created a world that only they were privy to.

Readily able to read between the lines, Scott cut in, "Hey! I'm starved. Why don't I just take a quick run to the shopping mall down the road and pick us up something to eat?"

"Yeah. Why don't you do that?" Braxton mumbled absently, never taking his eyes off Tempest.

Scott smiled a knowing smile, shrugged his shoulders, and sauntered off.

"Tempest." He barely spoke her name, but the sound of his voice drew her out of the enchanted spell. He stepped toward her.

"Please, don't," she whispered. But all the while her heart said yes.

She reminded him of a frightened doe, frozen with fear but ready to dash away at any sudden movement. He took another cautious step forward.

She turned away and moved to the right.

He stepped closer until he left her no room at all, their bodies only inches apart.

She felt his hot breath on her exposed neck, and a shiver of wanting ran through her. She knew she should move away, run as far as she could, but she couldn't.

He lowered his head to her neck and placed a gentle kiss behind one ear and then the other. An almost indiscernible sigh escaped her lips, but she did not move. Ever so slowly he ran his hands tenuously up her arms until they reached her shoulders, his caress a subtle command.

Gathering her into his arms, he held her snugly against the hard lines of his body. The unspeakable pleasure of holding her once again made him shudder with joy. For countless seconds he held her that way, enjoying the contact, the scent of her, the feel of her skin against his face. He buried his face in her hair, moaning her name over and over again.

He spun her to face him, as his instincts told him that she might spring from his hold at any moment. So in one forward motion, before she had time to resist, he locked her in his arms, his gaze riveted on her face, searching for any hint of doubt.

She felt powerless to resist as she looked up into ebony eyes, her heart thudding madly. The anticipation made her dizzy with longing, even though her mind raced with countless reasons as to why she should pull away, stop this thing—this crazy, frightening, exciting thing that flamed between them—before it was too late. But he had opened that secret room in her heart, and the floodgates of desire rose rapidly, sweeping her away with its force.

Then slowly and seductively his gaze swept downward from her eyes and rested on her parted lips.

She felt her knees weaken, and as if in slow motion his mouth descended onto hers.

Shockwaves of pleasure shot through her as his sweet lips burned against hers like a torch—as he moved his mouth over hers in slow drugging kisses. Tears of pure bliss christened her eyes when his velvet tongue parted her lips, causing a quake of desire to erupt and explode within her.

He tantalized her with his tongue, and between every kiss he breathlessly ground out her name, reaffirmed his love, apologized for her hurt.

Her mind spun in ecstasy at the pleasure that he had reawakened in her, and she clung to him, relishing every breathtaking second, yielding to the domination of his lips and his words.

Growing more bold, and spurred on by her acquiescence, his hands moved gently down the length of her spine then slid up under her sweater. She held her breath in expectation, just as they heard a car horn blow.

They quickly sprang apart like high school sweethearts caught in the backseat of an old Chevy. They looked at each other, merriment flashing in their eyes. The ridiculousness of their behavior shook them both with silent laughter.

Tempest began to giggle, softly at first and then building with each second. Braxton, caught up in the silken euphoria of the moment, joined her, until they were both doubled over, tears streaming down their faces.

"Well, I'm glad you two are enjoying your-selves," Scott exclaimed, stepping in and depositing a huge bag of burgers and sodas on the wooden table. "I just hope ya'll are as hungry as you are happy."

For the moment, Tempest thought between fits of laughter, *only for the moment.* But she slept that night in a deep peace for the first time in years, looking forward to tomorrow with hope.

They were cautious once again with each other after that—both fearing yet wanting to be alone. But with so much to accomplish in a short span of time, they hardly had the opportunity to dwell on themselves. The next two days flew by, and as the week came to a rapid close, Tempest knew that these magic moments had to end. Tomorrow David would be home and this fantasy world of romance and secret liaisons would cease.

Scott had just gone out to load up the car, leav-ing Tempest and Braxton alone for the first time since that fateful afternoon.

"We got a lot accomplished, don't you think?" Tempest asked, purposely avoiding looking at him as she nervously stuffed sketches and pens into her bag.

Braxton leaned against the table, his arms fold-ed, his eyes raking her body, drinking in these last moments. He made no attempt to hide the fact that he was watching her.

"There's still a lot more to be done. You know that, don't you?" he said huskily.

She felt a heated rush at his words and read his

meaning. She turned quickly away to hide her anxiety, alarmed at the magnitude of her own desire.

"Well, of course. There's—"

But before she could finish, he had spun her around and captured her in his arms. His mouth pressed down hot and demanding on hers. She tried in vain to break free of his powerful hold, but his arms were like vises, and she was held helplessly in his grip.

"I'm not going to let you go," he breathed in her ear. "Not again." His mouth swept down hungrily to recapture hers, and her resolve flew off with the late afternoon breeze as she gave in to the pounding temptation of his kiss. Then he moved slightly back but would not release her fully. He looked down at her with such sweet tenderness, a sensuous light brightening his eyes.

"I want you as much as I know you want me," he said. "We love each other. What we feel can't be wrong." Reality slapped her hard. What in the world was she doing? After he walked off into the sunset, what would she have—another bag of memories? She pulled forcefully from his grip.

"I can't take back what's already happened between us. But I can stop it here. I have a life, Braxton. I can't do this." Her voice was almost a plea. "You don't honestly expect me to risk it all for a romantic interlude with you?"

"I do," he said softly. "Because I know we're worth the risk." He spoke those simple words with the conviction of a man who could no longer be satisfied with a mere dream.

"But—"

"Shhh." He pressed a finger to her lips. "I don't want this day to end, baby, not yet, not now—not ever."

Just then Scott pushed through the doors. "You guys ready? I'm all packed up."

"You go ahead," Braxton said as his eyes held Tempest's. "I'll meet you back at the hotel. Tempest has agreed to drive me back." There was an intimate pleading in his gaze that she knew she could no longer resist.

"I'll see you on Monday, Scott," she said in a faraway voice.

He paused to look at them, shaking his head in wonderment. But they had already forgotten he was there. He made a hasty exit and was off. *So much for my advice*, he thought.

✕

Braxton took her hand in his. "Let's go for a walk," he urged softly. She nodded her response.

The late afternoon sun was still warm on their faces. They strolled silently through the expanse of the complex to the wooded area beyond. Coming to a lake embraced by blooming trees and budding grass, they stopped. He turned to her, holding her captive with his look. "I've never stopped thinking about you. You were always with me in my heart."

He eased her down onto the grass and sat beside her. His strong fingers trailed across her face, recommitting every line, every curve to his memory.

Where was her anger, her hurt, her commitment to her husband? She lost it all whenever she looked into his eyes. How could she combat what she knew was imminent, when his look took her breath away? It didn't matter that she didn't have the answers to their ill-fated past. She didn't know if she even cared. She knew only that if she let this moment slip away, she might never have this time of happiness again.

She leaned up and touched his lips softly with her own in response.

"Let me hold you, baby. I need to feel you next to me," he whispered.

He pulled her into his arms, drowning in the fresh scent of her hair, burying his face in its cottony softness. She in turn melted in his hold, the contact sending electric waves through her body.

He tilted up her chin and brought his lips down to meet hers. She trembled and he pulled her ever closer, pressing his body firmly against hers.

Tentatively his moist tongue traced the outline of her opened lips, savoring their candy sweetness. His hands stroked her body, igniting the embers that lay just beneath the surface.

In unison her fears and doubts began to resurface, arching upward until they neared the exterior of her consciousness. But just as swiftly they were relinquished as he brought his lips to her neck, gliding his tongue along the distended muscles. She couldn't fight it and instead she slowly touched his arms, his back, and ran her fingers through the exposed hair on his chest, making him shudder with the feathery lightness of her touch. He let out a soft moan of delight and taunted her mouth further with his own.

"Braxton," she breathed. He barely heard the whisper so enthralled was he by his mounting passion. "I want you. Make love with me."

His heart soared and spiraled to the heavens at the sweet surrender of her doubts. Like a treasured jewel he laid her on her back, his body next to hers.

His fingers reached out and caressed her face, traced a path across her neck, and disappeared under her open-collared blouse, seeking out the mounds that rose and fell seductively toward him.

She groaned at his touch and reached over to pull him onto her, her mouth melting into his.

With infinite slowness he methodically unbuttoned her blouse, enchanted by the nakedness which confronted him. He was stunned by her beauty. Her coppery skin glowed, and he buried his head between the heaving loveliness of her breasts. First one then the other, his tongue circled and tasted the soft sweetness of her hardening nipples. She moaned and cooed at his touch, pushing herself against his mouth.

He wanted to explore her further but hesitated, wary of her fragile state of mind. But her slender fingers took possession of his hand and pressed it to her, freeing him of any remaining reservations.

He slipped his hand under her skirt and freed her of her clothing beneath. Her thighs trembled at his touch, but she urged him on.

"Please touch me," she groaned in a throaty whisper, no longer able to contain her own growing need.

Knowing fingers sought out her hidden cavity. He let out a spontaneous moan of pleasure to find the dewy welcome. He pressed his finger against her, eliciting her cry of absolute surrender. Her hips arched against the taunting of his hand as she writhed beneath him, drenching him in her rising arousal.

She slowly, cautiously, unbuttoned his shirt. Then she grew bolder and loosened the buckle of his pants. "I want to know you again—feel you," she murmured.

Braxton leaned on his side, giving her easy access to what she desired. She freed him and a gasp slipped from her lips when what she sought rose majestically before her. With sure fingers she took him in her grasp.

"Tempest...baby," he groaned as he sucked in air through his teeth. He was hardly able to speak. His voice became a rumble as he savored the sensations of her touch.

Her fingers stroked him, leaving her shaking with the throbbing power that she held in her hand. Her mouth sought out his nipples and she fondled them with her tongue.

He was barely able to contain his mounting desire. He had held himself in check, but now he knew that she was ready. Turning her onto her back, he removed the rest of her clothing, laying her bare before his eyes. Lowering himself he found her breasts once again. She let out a moan of erotic pleasure to his ears as his tongue made contact with her taut nipples. His hands prepared her body for him, as he saturated them in her essence.

Slowly his tongue traced a searing path down her body, hovering over her quivering stomach. Gradually he eased further down, savoring every inch of her. Her velvety thighs tightened, but he gently separated them with a careful hand.

"Just relax," he whispered. "I only want to love all of you.

"Oh, Braxton—"

He had reached her core. Her hips rose in spasmodic response as he searched further. She began to whimper like a baby, rocking and shuddering under the intense sensations he created within her.

He drank of her like a vintage wine, rocketing in the potency of her wild abandon. His own need was growing beyond endurance, but he would not release her, delving even further into her center. He could feel her rising excitement as her thighs tightened around him. She reached down and urged him deeper into her realm, straining against him for fulfillment.

Then with painstaking slowness, he rose above her, his eyes burning into hers, trying desperately to hold on to the control that was fast slipping away from him. He watched her tremble beneath him.

"I won't hurt you, stormy one," he whispered. "I'll never hurt you again."

"I'm not afraid."

Again his lips came down on hers in a fiery kiss. Reaching under her, he pulled her hips to meet his manhood. He pressed against her gently, then with more force as the welcoming depths of her body beckoned him. She felt the building pressure and let out a muted cry just as he found his home within her warmth. The honeyed sheath expanded to encompass the length and breadth of him. He hovered immobile, drawing in the surreal pleasure of the satiny feel of her. The heat of passion nearly threw him over the edge of sublime surrender, but he held back, wanting this beauty that they shared to last forever.

As a ship at sea, they rolled and soared with the waves of their pent-up desire. Time stood still while they searched the universe, finding an unimaginable ecstasy in their union. As one, they traveled to a world they thought they would have never found again.

She was everything—more than he had dreamed of, or remembered. He was the culmination of all the love she had locked inside of her—a love she had believed was lost to her forever.

She called his name dozens of times, clinging to him with a ferocity that propelled him deeper.

They raced onward with the raging tide of passion, as it built to a fevered pitch, tossing them mercilessly against the waiting shore. The storm of the open sea rolled in. The clouds filled to their limits, threatening to explode and drench the land beneath.

He felt the tightening around him—the involuntary gripping that begged for release. Tears sprang from the corners of her eyes and the roaring waters rose to engulf her. She arched wildly against him, her head thrashing back and forth against the cool earth. Braxton was pushed beyond reason, watching the total surrender of her being.

"Look at me," he commanded, his voice a muffled growl.

Her eyes fluttered open, misty and unfocused. Her thoroughly kissed lips parted. She was unable to speak, but her eyes held his in unspoken promise.

He rose slowly above her, easing himself out from the warmth of her liquidy chasm, hovering at the very edge, wanting to relish those final moments. Then no longer able to withstand the bittersweet denial, he plunged to the hilt, hurtling them over the barriers of time and space.

"Braxton!" His name echoed throughout the corners of his mind, soaring over the clouds as they dove and ascended to blinding, breath-stopping rapture. They lay still in each other's arms, comforted by the nearness, and the last thing she recalled before drifting off into a satiated sleep was that she had never been so happy, felt so thoroughly loved, or been so frightened.

Chapter Nine

Caught between the conscious and the unconscious, Tempest slowly pulled herself up through the hypnotic effect of what had to be the most magnificent dream she had ever experienced. However, when her eyes fluttered open to see the radiance of the setting sun painted across the horizon, and felt the steady breathing and a muscled arm draped possessively across her hip, she knew that finally her dream had come true. The past six years of believing that everything was perfect in her life had been one long illusion. This was reality—lying next to the man that she loved beyond reason.

She sighed a sigh of deep contentment, when the veracity of her situation hit her like a speeding train. She came fully awake.

What on earth had she done? She'd committed the cardinal sin. What was worse was that it was with the very man who had turned her life upside down and left her once before. What she had allowed to happen was just what she had been battling against from the first moment she'd laid eyes on him again.

How could she have been so stupid? Was she so starved for affection that she would give herself so willingly to him? She'd allowed herself to be used. She'd fallen for the words of love that she had so wanted to hear. He couldn't love her, not the way that she loved him. If he did, he would have never abandoned her when she needed him the most. Where were the words of love then?

This time she'd walk away from him before he hurt her again. There was no way that she was going to believe that hurt wasn't in the cards.

She gently eased from his hold, ashamed of her weakness, angry at herself and at him. He felt her stir next to him and he slowly opened his eyes and was filled with such joy at the realization that she was finally his again. Everything would work out. He just knew that it would. Now that she had willingly given herself to him and they were bound together again in a physical union, he felt confident that he could get her to understand what had happened.

"Hello, beautiful," he whispered. He reached out for her, wanting to savor her warmth next to him.

She shrugged away from him, covering herself with her discarded blouse.

"What's wrong?" He sat up, startled.

"I've got to go," she said, her voice cold as ice.

A knot twisted in his stomach. He could under-stand her having feelings of guilt, but not her reaction to him. Not after what they had shared.

"Just like that? 'I've got to go?'" His voice turned hard with the panic that was slowly forming.

"Listen, Braxton." Her eyes took on a steely glint. "I was a fool once, and I paid for it. Lord knows I paid. But I won't be a fool again. This was a mis-take—one that I would like to put behind me as quickly as possible." She tossed her unbound hair behind her shoulder, as if to punctuate her point.

"A mistake?" He couldn't believe what he was hearing. "How on earth could you think that this was—"

"If you want that ride back to the city, I suggest that you get dressed." She spun away from him, and hurriedly put on her clothes, fighting desperately against the tears that threatened her facade of indifference.

The twenty-minute ride back into Manhattan was conducted in tension-filled silence—both of them needing to speak but afraid of saying the wrong thing. As the Hilton Hotel loomed into view, Braxton knew that any attempt at salvaging this fragile relationship would have to be done now.

The car screeched to a halt, and Tempest stared straight ahead, afraid that if she looked at his departing figure, her resolve would crumble. Seconds passed, but he didn't move. Her heart pounded in her chest. *Why won't he just get out and get this over with? Can't he see that I'm only holding on by a thread? Please don't say anything. I couldn't bear it.* She gripped the steering wheel to keep her hands from shaking.

"I wrote to you," he began softly. "For months I wrote to you. You never answered my letters." Pain outlined his simple words.

A somersault shot through her stomach. No! She wouldn't believe that. It couldn't be true.

"Stop it! Just stop it!" She covered her ears to block out the lies. "Why would you say such a thing? You never wrote to me! You never called!" Her voice rose in indignation and anguish, filling the car with all the anger she could release while still withholding her tears.

He twisted around in his seat and grabbed her shoulders with such force that it caused her teeth to clamp shut.

"Now you listen to me." His voice was low and threatening. "I've never lied to you. Do you understand that?" He shook her slender frame, bringing his point home.

"My father died. We lost the house, his business was going down the tubes. My life was in chaos. My letters explained everything. But I never heard from you. Some of them came back unopened. Some of them never came back."

"So what are you saying?" she asked defiantly. "Are you saying that I *ignored* your letters, that it's my fault?"

"I don't know what happened, sweetheart," he said, loosening his hold. "All I do know is that some horrible joke has wreaked havoc on our lives." His eyes pleaded with her to believe him. "And then when I finally located your grandmother's phone number, she kept saying that you didn't want to talk to me. I kept calling until one day I called and the number was changed."

"What? She never told—" Her mind raced back to those early days. Those calls that her grandmother always claimed were wrong numbers. Could he possibly be telling the truth? But if Braxton wasn't lying to her, then her grandmother had. That she refused to believe.

"Never told you what?" he demanded, the bud of expectation inching through his voice.

"She never told me anything because it never happened," she stated flatly, her eyes fixed straight ahead. "Now would you please get out of my car. I have a family to tend to."

"Oh, you mean that loving, iceberg of a husband?" he spat out sarcastically.

"No." She spun to face him. "Our...my daughter." Oh God, what had she said?

He stared at her in momentary disbelief. Then he asked softly, "You have a daughter?" His voice was filled with wonderment and a new admiration. Yet another empty space opened up in his heart. He had so hoped that one day they would have a child together—it had been his dream; a daughter in the image of his only love.

"I'm happy for you," he said at last. "I had always hoped—"

"Braxton, don't." She put up her hand to forestall any further comments and breathed a silent sigh of relief. *He didn't notice,* she assured herself, thankful for the reprieve.

Agreeing reluctantly, he reached for the door handle, then stopped. He turned back to her, his eyes boring into her averted face. "I was sorry to hear about your grandmother. I hope she'll be all right. If you believe nothing else, believe this, Tee...I love you and I'll be there if you need me. Just like I've always been. Ask your grandmother."

With that he stepped from the car with the grace of a jungle tiger—his portfolio under one arm, his denim jacket slung over the opposite shoulder—and disappeared into the lobby of the hotel before she could respond. *I didn't get to tell you how sorry I am about your father,* she called out from her heart.

For several moments she sat motionless in the car with her arms bracing the steering wheel, her head resting on its cool leather. Too much was happening. Her head throbbed with the tension of the past half-hour. The inference of what Braxton had said left her stunned with incredulity. If what he said was true, then her grandmother was at the root of it all. But she couldn't be. Her soul cried out in agony at the possibility. *Not Gram, not my Gram.*

She spent a fitful night, filled with dreams of all the people whom she loved and trusted turning against her. Most of all, she saw Braxton's eyes, and a secret part of her wanted to believe what she saw in them. Yet if she did, the foundation on which she had built her life had been one big lie.

For the next few weeks, Tempest played the role of the devoted wife, the first-rate businesswoman, the loving granddaughter, and supermom. She made appearances with David at conferences and talk shows. She poured all of her energy into assisting him in his campaign, working on the designs for two of the model apartments at the complex, running back and forth to the hospital, and spending the time in between with her daughter. Which left her no time or energy to dwell on her own problems.

She saw very little of Braxton, which was just as well as far as she was concerned. She always made sure that she was at the complex when he was not. When they did see each other, it was across the conference table, headed by her husband. But she hadn't forgotten his words, and they haunted her as she walked down the long hospital corridor to her grandmother's room.

Ella had slowly begun to come out of her coma. She'd drifted in and out of consciousness for the past several days, but never spoke or stayed awake for any length of time. However, Tempest had received an urgent call from the hospital, just an hour prior, stating that her grandmother had finally spoken and had asked to see her right away.

As she entered the hushed hospital room and saw the now fragile figure before her, the doubts that she had harbored about her Gram dissolved like grains of sugar in a pitcher of lemonade. There was no way that this loving, unselfish woman could have so blatantly destroyed her chance at happiness. She just couldn't have done that.

She slowly approached Ella's bedside—the soft brushing of her calf-length leather skirt the only sound—just as her eyes fluttered open and rested on Tempest.

"Hi, Gram," she whispered, her eyes lit with happiness and love. Ella reached out a wrinkled hand and motioned Tempest closer to her.

Her voice was strained and weak, but the words she spoke had more force than the fury of nature let loose on the open plain.

"I don't want you to say anything, baby girl. I just want you to listen and listen good. I don't know how much time I have," she said weakly, "but I know I have to make my peace."

Thirty minutes later uncontrolled tears streamed down Tempest's eyes and stained her jade-colored silk blouse. Her slender figure rocked with the force of her sobs. She locked her arms around her body as if to squeeze the pain away.

How could this be? She wanted to reach up to the heavens and snatch back the time she had lost, vent her anger and pain at the ones who were responsible. But she couldn't do that, because deep inside she knew that as twisted as it all was, Ella did it out of love for her.

"I wouldn't blame you if you hated me," Ella wheezed. "It took nearly dyin' for me to realize that there may only be one chance in life to truly love someone, and I had taken that chance away from you."

"Gram, I could never hate you." Tempest sniffed as she looked on Ella. "I know—"

"You just hush and listen, 'cause you don't know." Ella's body was racked with a fit of coughing before she could continue.

"When I got pregnant with your mama, and her daddy ran off, my family abandoned me. I was a black sheep, someone to be ashamed of. I had to leave Alabama, and I came up north. I stayed in rented rooms for weeks at a time until my money ran out, and then I did housework for whoever would hire me. I scrubbed floors, washed windows, and cleaned folks' dirty clothes by hand. 'Cause I knew that I had to provide for my baby". Tears rolled down Ella's now gaunt cheeks at the memories.

Tempest reached out and took her grandmother's hand and pressed it against her cheek. "Oh, Gram, you don't have to tell me all of this."

"Yes, I do. You deserve to know the whole

truth."

✂

There was too much to comprehend. She forced herself to keep her mind on her driving. She'd already spoken to Bridgette, half hysterical, half filled with joy. Bridgette promised to meet her as soon as she could get away so that "I can get a coherent statement and make sure that you haven't lost your lid," she had said, overjoyed for her friend.

A montage of events floated through Tempest's brain, as the Mercedes sped down the highway headed for her secret hideaway at Shady Point. But one thing remained clear and undistorted; Braxton had told her the truth. That realization lifted a weight from her soul that had been with her since the day she left Virginia.

She turned right at the next intersection and headed toward her exit. As she entered her exit ramp, she recalled how she'd found the inn quite by mistake about four years earlier. She'd been lost when she stumbled on it tucked away in a cove of trees, surrounded by a natural lake. She'd fallen in love with the homey atmosphere and the hearty cuisine, and she made a point of coming often ever since, especially when she had a lot on her mind.

The innkeeper had come to recognize her as she became a regular guest. It had gotten to a point that whenever she stayed over with her daughter, she would

137

be given special treatment and the same room over-looking the lake.

She'd beat Bridgette there by at least an hour, she thought, her mind whizzing back to the present as she made her final turn. That would give her some time alone to think through what she must do. One thing was certain, she thought, as she pulled up in front of the Shady Point Inn. She must leave David, for her own salvation before they wound up destroying each other.

Now as she stepped through the heavy oak doors, she received an effusive welcome from the pro-prietors.

"Our little Tempest is here, Sophie," boomed Herbert.

"Come, come...let me get you the special of the day. Clam chowder," he said, clamping a fleshy arm around Tempest's shoulder.

This was just what she needed, she thought, as she returned the enthusiastic greeting—a little bit of pampering.

"So," Herbert said with a mock frown on his rosy face, "where is our little munchkin?"

Tempest threw her head back in laughter. "She's home with my housekeeper, Clara."

"You must bring her on your next visit," admonished Sophie from behind the counter.

"I certainly will. Now how about that clam chowder? I'm starved." She grinned, feeling truly happy for the first time in a long while.

"So Gram believed that David could provide for me the way that Braxton couldn't," Tempest said as she sat facing Bridgette. "She was so wrapped up in making sure that I was secure and well taken care of, it totally clouded her judgment. She just set out to keep Braxton out of my life."

"She must have had a really hard time raising your mother," Bridgette said.

"I don't think that was all of it." She looked down into her bowl of soup and absently stirred as she spoke. "I think that because my grandfather had abandoned her, and she had put all her faith and hope in loving him, she just couldn't believe that relationships could be built on love. Then when my father ran out on my mother and never married her, that just reconfirmed her feelings."

"So before your mom died, she made your grandmother promise to make the best life possible for you."

"Yes." Her faint smile held a hint of sadness. "That best life in my grandmother's eyes was David. My grandmother had struggled to raise my mother and then struggled to raise me since I was two years old. David was the means to the end of that struggle for both of us."

"Then it stands to reason that David had his own motivations as well," Bridgette said, taking a sip of tea.

"Initially I honestly believed that David truly cared about me. But David is a strange man. He suffered a lot in his youth, and I think along the road his morals and his humaneness got distorted. I must admit though," she said in a faraway voice, "he really swept me away when we first met at the design show at Parsons School of Design. Then when I returned from Virginia, an emotional wreck, he was there. I'll always be grateful to him for that no matter whatever else he may have done."

"So what are you going to do? And what about Kai? What are you going to tell her about her father?"

"First, I've got to talk with David and let him know how I feel about our marriage. He has to see that it can't continue this way. Then I'll talk with Braxton, and tell him everything. Maybe he'll find room in his heart to forgive me for being such a blind fool all of these years."

She took a deep breath. "As for Kai—" She hesitated. "I hope that between myself and her father we'll be able to help her to understand and make the transition. I know it's going to be hard, but we'll just have to work it through. After that, I'll just have to take it one day at a time. The outcome of the election will weigh heavily on what I do. My conscience won't let me just walk out on David, not after all he's done for me."

"Don't you mean *to* you?" Bridgette asked with a sarcastic smirk.

"Bridgette," she sighed in exasperation, "be fair. A lot of what I have today I owe to David."

Bridgette leaned forward on her elbows and stared directly into Tempest's eyes. "That may be true, but you did one helluva lot of it on your own. You built that business. It's your designs that have the clients raving. I think it's about time you started thinking about you for a change, instead of building your whole life around what you owe other people." She reached out and touched her hand. "Don't you?"

Tempest took both of Bridgette's hands in hers. "You know what? I've been thinking the exact same thing myself." A smile spread slowly across her lips, as the thought brought new hopefulness and brightened her spirits.

❧

It was well after nine o'clock when she returned home. The house was quiet as she paced the floor like a caged tigress, planning what she would say to David when he came in. He'd called while she was out, leaving a message that he would be in around ten. She checked her gold Longine watch, a present from David the previous Christmas, and realized with a start that he would be walking through the door any minute. Her heart thudded in her chest while she twisted and un-twisted her hands as she paced. Maybe she should just forget the whole thing and just try to work things out between them. She shook her head against that thought. That was an impossibility, she scolded herself. The distance between them was too wide to bridge. David was no longer the man she married, and neither was she the same woman.

Unable to withstand the tension of waiting any longer, she flipped on the stereo and curled up on the couch. At least the music would block out the maddening silence and muffle the confusion that was running rampant in her head. Music had always had the power to soothe her body and relax her spirit, and it wasn't long before she felt herself begin to unwind. She could feel herself drifting off to the mellow sounds of her favorite jazz pianist, when David came through the door. She sat straight up in the chair as if hit with an electric shock

"Well, I didn't expect to find you awake," David said, tossing his coat in the first available chair. "Join me in a nightcap?" He headed toward the bar and began preparing himself a glass of brandy.

"No...thank you," she mumbled. A surge of apprehension shot through her, but she knew what she must do. She slowly rose from her seat.

"David, we have to talk."

He put the glass to his lips, tossed his head back and emptied the contents. "Do we?" he asked, his voice laden with sarcasm. "About what?" He turned to place his drained glass on the bar counter, then slowly turned to face her, his eyes cold and challenging.

"About us," she answered with quiet firmness. "I want out of this marriage, David." She stood resolutely before him. "It's not working. I'd be willing to stick with you through the election, but after that then—"

"I, on the other hand, think this marriage is working just fine," he stated flatly, unmoved by her request. He folded his arms and stared at her through emotionless eyes. "You see, my dear *wife*," he said, as he stepped down from the raised platform and strolled around the expanse of the large foyer. "We are the perfect public couple. You give stability and credence to me in the public's eye. They see us as a team, working for the common good. And you, my dear"—his voice hard and exact—"are a part of my team. I do not let go of my team members until I am ready."

"David, listen to me." She moved toward him, her voice marking her disbelief at his words. "I'm not one of your pawns in a business game. You have to let me go. I don't love you." Regret rimmed her voice. "Not like I once did. I cannot live in a loveless marriage. I'll help you any way that I can. I promise you that." Her eyes begged him to understand.

"You'll be what I want you to be for as long as I want you to be. Do you honestly think that because Braxton Thorne has re-entered your life that you can suddenly pull out?" His voice rose in accusation.

She stepped back, stunned that he knew.

He gave a menacing chuckle. "So you thought I

didn't know. The first mistake I made was not having him investigated before I requested his services. However, I always correct my mistakes. I know everything. Do you understand, *everything."* His eyes held a fiendish glare.

She willed herself not to reach across the short space and smack the smug look of triumph off his smooth features. She felt violated by his inquiries into her past. Now all that she had held sacred and secret within her heart was spread out before him on some dossier. If that's the way he wanted to play this game, then there was no sense in her attempting to mollify the situation. She drew on all of her strength, her eyes conveying the disdain within her.

"You do what you want, David. Since you know everything, there's no point in continuing this charade." She thrust her chin out in defiance. "I've reconsidered my offer to remain with you through the election. I'll have my lawyer contact you in the morning." She spun around and headed toward the bedroom.

His voice reached out to her like an invisible claw, and held her dangling in the grip of his words. "If you so much as think for a minute that I'll let you divorce me, then you haven't learned much about me. The moment I receive anything even smelling like a divorce action, I will have my lawyer institute a custody action to take Kai away from you."

She whirled around at his words. Her voice shot across the room like a missile. "You wouldn't dare."

"Why of course I would, and I'd win, after I have you proven unfit—and an adulteress." He looked down at his nails. "I'll pull all of your clients away, and you won't even have the money to fight me in court. When I'm finished with you, I will ruin your Mr. Thorne. He'll never work in architecture again. You know I can do it, and I will if I must. The decision is yours."

Sheer panic ripped through her. Words escaped her. She could risk losing anything—her business, her happiness—but not her daughter. Never Kai!

Certainly Braxton didn't deserve what David was capable of doing to him. She felt defeated. The prospect of her future brought a sudden chill to her body that felt like ice water running through her veins.

"So, my darling wife, I believe this conversation is ended." He strolled out of the apartment and was gone.

She stood there for countless moments, paralyzed. She tried to hold on to her last bit of control, but her torment was too deep—it became physical pain. She closed her eyes against the onslaught of her agony, as burning tears rolled unchecked down her high cheeks.

She fell into the chair, as her knees threatened to buckle beneath her. What was she going to do? She was trapped, and there seemed to be no way out. Must she pay for the rest of her life for what she did? Was she not deserving of some happiness in life? She wept aloud, the sobs rocking her body.

She had overestimated her opponent. She had to attributed to him qualities like compassion, understanding, even forgiveness, all of which he no longer seemed to possess. Was she the cause of that as well? She didn't know anymore. Where was the man she had married? Her thoughts crashed about in a maelstrom of guilt and confusion, then came to a grinding halt of realization.

If there was anyone who could help now, it was Braxton! A momentary sense of calm and an inkling of hope swept through her. She drew back her tears and wiped away the traces with the back of her hand. She would go to him with the whole twisted story, she decided, and together they would find a way to combat this plague that had been set against them.

Optimism lighted her eyes, and the anxiety of waiting until morning was more than she could handle. She couldn't risk losing another moment.

As she slid into her car, it began to pour. However, she drove with a single-minded purpose, oblivious to the pounding rain and earth-shaking thunder. All she could think of was getting to Braxton—of having him hold her in his arms and assure her that everything would be all right. She had so much to tell him, so much that she had hidden that he deserved to know. But most of all to tell him that she loved him, had never stopped and never would.

Just the short hop from the curb to the revolving

doors of the hotel left her drenched. Stopping briefly at the front desk, she asked for his room number and headed for the elevators marked 20-30. The fleeting thought ran through her head that she must look like a wet rag doll but it was quickly discarded when she visualized seeing him again.

Riding in the cushioned elevator, her heart was the only sound to be heard, as it thudded wildly in anticipation. The short walk down the carpeted hallway seemed an eternity, and her heart beat faster with every approaching step. She raised a tremulous hand to knock on the door, but stopped in midair. Conflicting thoughts ran through her head. What if he couldn't help her? What if he told her to get out of his life for keeping the fact that... No, he wouldn't do that, she assured herself. If nothing else, Braxton was a forgiving man, and he would forgive her—of that she was sure. She took a calming breath and knocked. The door was opened almost instantly. Standing before her, bare-chested and breathtaking was Braxton, astonishment etched across his face and defining his voice.

"Tempest?"

Her eyes lit up at the sight of him, and a warm smile easily found its way to her lips. Momentarily she forgot what she was supposed to say, as she fell under the enchanted spell of his eyes. Then a voice from behind him reached over his shoulder and struck her as solidly as a brick.

"Well, I heard that New Yorkers stayed out late,"

came the honeyed drawl. "I guess it must be true." Braxton turned, cold fury lighting his eyes, but giving Tempest a view to the person behind the voice.

A tremor of foreboding trickled up her spine when she laid eyes on the face that she had long ago banished to the back of her mind. She stood frozen, absorbing the implications of this woman's presence. But nothing could have prepared her for the words that were hurled at her with such bottomless contempt and triumph.

"However, I nevah thought that decent, upstanding ladies visited other women's husbands in the middle of the night."

Jasmine moved forward in slow, fluid movements until her voluptuous form stood in the frame of the opened doorway. She reached up and placed a hand on Braxton's shoulder, followed by a possessive kiss on his cheek.

Tempest didn't see him recoil or see the look of glee light Jasmine's eyes. Nor did she hear him call her name over and over again as she blindly raced for the elevator.

Chapter Ten

Days later Tempest still reeled from the shock of her visit to Braxton. Hurt and humiliation hung around her heart and weighed her down like an anchor. She refused to answer any of Braxton's calls and had moved into the apartment's spare room to avoid David.

She went through the paces of her life in mechanical motion, totally removed from the world around her. It seemed that she had crawled inside of herself to find a safe and comfortable place in the dark corners of her mind. But she refused to cry and vowed never to cry again.

The only clue to life within her was demonstrated in her work. She worked long, grueling hours—not eating, sleeping little, but creating some of the most magnificent design details she had ever done.

Bridgette watched her, as day after day Tempest

slipped further away. She'd declined to talk with Bridgette about what had happened. But Bridgette was sure it must have been devastating to get Tempest in such a state. She'd never seen her so possessed, so obsessed with her work, and she knew this was Tempest's way of dealing with her hurt. She'd seen it before, but this time was different, more destructive. She knew that if she didn't do something soon, Tempest was going to break.

Finally, one morning, no longer able to stand by idly and watch Tempest eat herself alive, she decided to confront her.

Tempest was sitting at her drafting table when Bridgette burst into her office, slamming the door solidly behind her.

Tempest barely raised her head, looking at Bridgette with expressionless eyes. "How long is this going to go on?" Bridgette demanded, her hands planted firmly on her hips.

"I don't know what you're talking about," Tempest answered blandly.

Bridgette stormed over to the table, snatched the sketch pad and tossed it on the floor.

"You know perfectly well what I mean, Tempest," she railed. "Look at you. You're a wreck. You have circles under your eyes, and you've lost about five pounds. The whole office is buzzing about the change in you."

"I still don't know what you're talking about,"

she answered in the same flat voice, avoiding looking at Bridgette.

"I'm talking about you and what you're doing to yourself and everyone you come in contact with!"

"Bridgette, please," she begged. "I'm not in the mood for one of your lectures." She rose from her stool and stood facing the window.

"Well, that's just tough, because you're going to get one anyway."

"Just leave me alone," she whispered.

"I won't because I'm your friend. I don't know what happened, but you can't let it destroy you. You've never been someone who let adversity beat you down. Since when do you go cowering into a corner like some old lady afraid of the dark?"

"Leave me alone, Bridgette."

"So you're not going to fight back, just roll over and play dead?"

"I can't fight back," she said weakly.

Bridgette hurried to her side. "Of course you can," she assured. "You know you can."

Bridgette turned Tempest around to face her. She looked directly into her eyes.

"I'll help you, honey," she said softly. "If you'll just let me."

They started slowly, one then the other, until tears flowed freely in a continuous silent, cleansing stream. Bridgette held the stiff body, whispering comforting words, rocking her in her arms.

Tempest cried until she was spent and limp, and it was only then that Bridgette released her and ushered her to the couch, offering her a glass of spring water from the carafe.

"Here, drink this. You must be dehydrated by now." Bridgette gave her a teasing smile and was rewarded with a smile of gratitude in return.

Tempest reached out a hand to Bridgette. "I don't know how you put up with me." She sniffed. "But I'm glad that you do."

"We all have our crosses to bear. I just got lucky when I got you." She flashed her a warm grin.

"I guess you deserve an explanation," Tempest said at last.

"Only if you want to."

"I do."

With painstaking calm, Tempest spun out the events that had redefined her future, leaving out no details, and concluding with her encounter at the hotel.

When she'd finished, Bridgette slumped back in her chair temporarily speechless. All she could think of was tearing out of that office, stringing David up on the nearest lamppost and kicking Braxton and his wife all the way back to Virginia. But of course she couldn't do that. She was the rational one.

"So you see, Bridge, there isn't anything that I

can do. David will make sure of that...and Braxton finished the job."

"We know where David is coming from," Bridgette said, considering the options. "But have you spoken with Braxton?"

"No!" She jumped up from her seat. "I don't intend to speak with him. What could he possibly say to me? He used me," she said, her husky voice threaded with pain.

"You deserve an explanation, Tee, if nothing else. He owes you that much." Bridgette went to stand beside her, placing a gentle hand on her shoulder. "You've spent the past six years in limbo. Do you intend to finish out your life the same way?"

Tempest straightened her shoulders and took a deep breath.

"You're right." She turned to face Bridgette, the old spark back in her eyes. "And I'm going to get one," she said, determination strengthening her voice.

"Now that's the Tempest I know." Bridgette pulled her into her arms and gave her a reassuring hug. "So get to it! And fix your face. You're a mess!"

※

"Everything's just gone crazy, Scott," Braxton said in despair. "Jasmine showing up like that was the last thing I expected. I haven't spoken to her since I left Virginia."

"You should have told Tempest from the beginning," Scott admonished. "That was a lousy way for her to find out."

"The last thing I need to hear from you right now," Braxton growled, "is what I should have done." He jammed his hands into his pockets and paced the carpeted floor, his handsome face twisted into a frown. Then realizing that his outburst at Scott was unwarranted ,he turned and apologized.

"Listen, I'm sorry, man," he said, running a hand across his beard. "I know it's not your fault. It was my own stupidity." He slammed a fist into the wall. "I've really screwed things up this time."

"Now that we have that cleared up," Scott quipped sarcastically, "what are you going to do about it?"

"I've tried calling her, but she won't answer my calls." He threw his hands up in the air in frustration.

"Where's your head, B.J.? Forget calling. Just go over to her office and make her listen."

Braxton considered it for a moment, uncertainty clouding his features. He leaned his muscled frame against the wall.

"She'll probably have me thrown out, you know."

"That's quite possible."

"She'll probably tell me she doesn't want to ever set eyes on me again."

"Probably."

"She'll probably—"

"She could probably do a lot of things," Scott cut in, tired of the excuses. "But you'll never know if you don't talk to her. Now will you?"

Braxton flashed a smile of submission. "Okay, I give up. You're right."

"Again, I might add."

Braxton gave him a wry grin. "So now what?"

"So now you get showered and dressed, put on your best cologne, and go after your lady love."

"Thanks, Scott," Braxton said, his voice full of gratitude.

"Aw, come off the mushy stuff." Scott patted Braxton on the shoulder and pushed him toward the bathroom. "Let's get this show on the road. Where's Jasmine, by the way?" he called out to Braxton.

"I told her she was going to have to find someplace else to stay," he yelled over the rushing shower water. "With any luck she'll be out of here by tonight."

Jasmine sat cross-legged on the leather couch, impatiently tapping her foot while waiting for David to conclude his phone conversation. He'd promised her half of her money when she arrived. She'd been there a full week and hadn't seen a red cent. Her time was running out. If she didn't make a payment in the next ten days, she was finished. *He'd better have a damned good explanation,* she fumed. She'd kept her end of the bargain.

"Mrs. Thorne," David intoned as he replaced the receiver. "I'm sorry to have kept you waiting. I'm sure you're wondering about your payment."

Her cheeks flushed at the blatant implication of greed.

"Actually, I—"

David waved a hand in dismissal.

"I know all about you, Mrs. Thorne. You were at one time heiress to the St. Claire shipping lines. Weren't you?"

"Yes, but—"

"It's such a shame that you squandered your father's estate and have now resorted to pawning museum pieces." He shook his head in feigned sadness.

Jasmine jumped up from her seat, indignation heightening her voice.

"Mistah Lang, I didn't come here to be harassed by you."

"You're here, Mrs. Thorne, because you need me," he said smoothly. "Now, please have a seat."

She plopped down on the couch with an insolent huff.

"Your job here is to keep your husband away from my wife until this project and the election is over—and give her enough reason to stay away from him permanently."

"How am I supposed to do that? He practically

threw me out when I showed up. He told me just this morning that I had to find someplace else to stay."

"You're a resourceful woman, Mrs. Thorne. You'll think of something." He stepped around to his desk and removed an envelope from the drawer.

"I'm sure," he said, handing her the envelope, "that this first installment will give you some, shall we say, inspiration, as well as compensate you for any inconvenience."

"I'm sure it will," she replied with a conspiratorial smile, as she inserted the envelope into her snakeskin purse.

At that point David's intercom buzzed. He jammed his finger down on the flashing light.

"I thought I told you no interruptions, Annie," he growled into the phone.

"But Mr. Lang, you told me to remind you of your twelve o'clock lunch date with Mr. Ackerman at the 21 Club."

"All right," he snapped. "Send for my driver. I'll be down in a few minutes."

He looked up at Jasmine. "You'll have to excuse me, Mrs. Thorne. I have a previous appointment."

Jasmine rose and in deliberate slow motion smoothed her emerald green, suede dress over her voluptuous hips. Taking a compact from her purse, she checked her lipstick and patted her close-cropped curls in place. Satisfied, she snapped the compact shut and returned it to her purse.

Slowly raising her long lashes, she gazed upon David, invitation dancing in her eyes. She was pleased to discover that David's eyes were riveted on her. She flashed him her most alluring smile.

David cleared his throat, his composure momentarily shaken. He ran a hand down the length of his maroon silk tie and fastened the button on the double-breasted, steel gray jacket.

"I'm sure we'll see each other soon, Mr. Lang." She pursed her red lips seductively.

"You'll be contacted, Mrs. Thorne," he stated firmly, reassuming his business air. The last thing he needed was this woman on his heels, he thought with a shudder.

"Please call me Jasmine. All my friends do."

"When we become friends, Mrs. Thorne, then I'll think about it."

Her mouth twisted into a sour grin. She gave him a curt nod of her bobbed head and swayed toward the door.

✖

Muted conversation rose and fell throughout the lush dining room of the 21 Club. Waiters and waitresses hurried about carrying trays laden with high-priced cuisine, eager to please the elite clientele.

David was seated at his favorite banquette table surrounded by beveled glass on three sides. It always gave him a sense of privacy and removed him from the traffic of the busy restaurant. He had chosen the poached salmon, one of his favorite dishes, along with a freshly tossed salad and yellow rice with almonds. His order arrived simultaneously with the arrival of Joseph Ackerman.

Joe Ackerman could easily be mistaken for the neighborhood candy store shopkeeper. His full head of gray hair, stooped shoulders, pot belly, and hesitant way of speaking belied the cunning and business acumen that had propelled him to the top of his field.

Soil research and testing had mushroomed into a booming business over the past two decades, and Joe had been one of its pioneers. Developers from across the country sought out his expertise, and David Lang dealt with only the best.

"Joe." David stood and extended his hand. "Good to see you. Have a seat."

"I, uh, can't stay long. I, uh, brought you the revised reports." He gingerly removed the computerized printouts from his battered satchel, an Ackerman trademark.

David immediately reviewed the figures and percentages that spanned the pale green sheets with rapt concentration.

"Excellent job, Joe. I couldn't have done better myself." He gave a derisive chuckle.

"The Environmental Protection Agency will get a copy of these tomorrow."

"Good. These will be in perfect sync with my assured victory tonight. Those EPA guys play real hardball. We can't afford any slipups. You're sure these are foolproof."

Joe peered at David over wire-rimmed glasses. "You didn't hire me because I make mistakes, did you?"

David leaned forward. His voice lost its congenial tone and took on a hard edge. "There's no room in business for mistakes, especially my business."

Joe was not moved by the subtle threat. He'd covered his tracks. It was up to Lang to cover his.

"I'll take my money now," he said calmly.

David extracted a long manila envelope from his jacket pocket.

"I hope," he said, his left eyebrow lifting in inquiry, "that this will be sufficient?"

"I'm, uh, sure that it will be." Ackerman quickly plucked the envelope from David's fingers and deposited it into his breast pocket.

Promptly rising from his chair, he unconsciously smoothed his always rumpled suit.

"Good day, Mr. Lang. Our business is concluded." He gave David a short nod and ambled out of the restaurant. David returned to his meal, totally satisfied that everything was going according to plan.

As Joe made his way down the crowded streets of the city, he was momentarily consumed by the implications of what he had done. If it was ever discovered that he was involved in providing false reports documenting that land free of toxic waste, he would be ruined.

What did it matter anyway? The doctors said he had only six months left, and Lang had paid him well for his illicit services. This final payment would cover the inevitable hospital expenses and leave a comfortable cushion for his wife and son, the only two reasons why he would ever compromise his principles. At least this was money that the government couldn't seize as assets if this whole scheme blew up. For that he was thankful.

✄

Jasmine leaned back in her seat and took a sip of her vodka martini, thoroughly satisfied that she'd dined at the 21 Club. The food was excellent, but the conversation was even better.

So Lang thought that he could intimidate her with blackmail, did he? Now she had something she could use against him as well. She smiled smugly. He'd definitely have to up the price of her compensation.

As she eased herself out of her seat, she mused: *They really should make these glass partitions thicker. You just never knew who might be on the other side.*

Chapter Eleven

Alone now, Tempest momentarily had second thoughts about seeing Braxton, but the rational voice of Bridgette echoed in her head, urging her forward.

The first thing she had to do was change clothes. She certainly wouldn't make the impression that she wanted dressed in her flannel shirt and patchwork jeans. She had always made it a habit to keep an extra outfit or two in her office closet, and she had the perfect one for this occasion.

Taking the pantsuit from the closet, she headed for her private bathroom to change. But when she stood in front of the full-length mirror and took a good look at herself for the first time in days, she was appalled at what she saw. Bridgette was right. What must her staff think?

Under her eyes were dark circles. Her high cheekbones looked gaunt from not eating, and her usually lustrous hair was dull and lifeless. Although she was always slender, but well proportioned, her body now carried the beginning signs of neglect. She gave a slight shudder at what she had done to herself. This was going to take more than a change of clothes. This required a major overhaul.

She turned on the shower full blast, grabbed her shampoo and conditioner, and stepped in under the pulsating water, washing away the last traces of doubt. Rubbing her bath oil across her body, her heart skipped in triple time as she anticipated their meeting. She knew her temper and impatience tended to get in the way and never solved anything. She would force herself to stay calm, she vowed, as she rinsed out the conditioner and turned off the shower. This time she would give him a chance to explain his side and keep an open mind. After all, she had enough explaining to do herself.

Her stomach lurched at the prospect, but she knew that she must tell him everything, no matter how things turned out between them, or how painful it might be. It was finally time.

She quickly blow-dried her hair, powdered her body in *Eternity* and slipped into her outfit.

The lightweight knit, royal blue pantsuit was one of her favorite outfits. The suede patches, of the same color, on the padded shoulders gave the suit that extra bit of dash. She draped an oblong, multi-colored silk scarf around her neck and down her right shoulder to break up the solid color of the ensemble.

Satisfied, she added gold teardrop earrings, a three-inch-wide gold bangle, and black ankle-length suede boots. Her final step was her makeup, which she meticulously applied. She outlined her almond-shaped eyes with a midnight blue pencil, thickened her lashes with a stroke of mascara, and detailed her lips with burnt sienna lipstick.

She checked her watch, and her heart gave a twitch. It was almost noon, and she knew he usually left the site about one o'clock after reviewing the progress of the technicians. If she hurried and didn't run into any traffic, she should make it before he left for the day. She snatched up her long black suede coat from the brass coat rack, grabbed her bag, and dashed out the door.

Marsha's head jerked up from her work when Tempest rushed out of her office. Her eyes widened in pleasure at the transformation.

"You look lovely, Ms. Dailey," Marsha gushed.

A sunshine smile brightened Tempest's face.

"Thank you, Marsha. I'll be going out for a few hours. I'll call in for messages."

She headed for the door, then stopped and came back to Marsha's desk.

"Marsha," she said softly, leaning forward on Marsha's desk, "thanks for being so patient with me. I know I've been really difficult lately."

"Don't even mention it. We all have our moments."

"Thanks anyway." She smiled and strutted

down the corridor toward the elevators, turning the heads of her staff designers en route, all of whom breathed a sigh of relief that their leader was finally back.

She waited at the elevator for what seemed an eternity, watching the lighted dial creep slowly upward to her floor, her anxiety building with every second.

Finally the doors opened, and an instant thrill shot through her. "Braxton?"

"Tempest, I was just—"

"I was on my way to—"

They both started to laugh when they realized that they were both babbling at the same time.

"Beautiful ladies first," he conceded, his eyes dark and smoldering, his voice a pulsing throb.

He stepped from the elevator and gently moved her away from the flow of discharging passengers.

She looked up into his eyes, and her insides dissolved. He'd come to see her. Why else would he be here? Her very being was filled with elation. *Please let this work out,* she prayed.

"I was, uh, on my way to see you," she said hurriedly, the blood pounding in her ears as she spoke. She looked down at her boots and shifted her coat from one arm to the other, then peered up at him through sooty lashes.

"It seems that we're finally on the same wavelength, stormy one," he said, his voice full of relief, and the intimate smile that he radiated scorched her from head to toe. "Is there somewhere we can talk in private? There's so much I want to tell you," he said softly.

"There's a lot I have to tell you, too," she said in a throaty whisper. "We could go down to the coffee shop or my office, or—" Then an idea came to her. The perfect place.

"Did you drive?" she asked, excitement rippling through her voice.

"Yes, I did, but—"

"Good. I have the perfect spot. It's just out of the city. We could be there in a half-hour," she rushed on.

"I've got the time if you do." He smiled, his eyes raking over her.

She felt her knees go weak.

"I hope you can keep up. You'll have to follow my car." She pressed the button for the elevator and flashed him a mischievous grin.

⚜

When they arrived at the Shady Point Inn, there was only one other couple, so they had their choice of seats. They chose a table in the far corner of the spacious room.

Braxton took a quick assessment of the setting. The heavy-beamed rafter ceiling and hardwood floors gave him a sense of being transported to an old English pub.

The early afternoon sunshine beamed in through the stained glass windows and bounced off the brass mugs that hung on the walls throughout the room, giving the dining area a rainbow quality.

"This is a beautiful place," he said finally.

"It's my secret hideaway."

They stared into each other's eyes, saying so much without a word being spoken.

"Look at that, Sophie," Herbert said to his wife, as he looked at the couple from behind the counter.

"Isn't it beautiful? There's nothing like two young people in love."

Herbert leaned over and planted a wet kiss on Sophie's rosy cheek. "Or two old people," he chuckled.

Tempest reached across the round oak table and placed a hand tentatively atop Braxton's. "I was so wrong about so many things, B.J."

"What do you—"

"Please, just let me get it all out," she cut in, "before I lose my nerve." She gave him a weak smile, then continued. "All these years," she said slowly, "I believed that you had abandoned me, until my grandmother told me the truth."

"Your grandmother?"

"She never told me about your calls or your letters. Just like you said. I never got any of them."

"But why?"

"You see, before I came to the University of Virginia, I'd met David at a design show. He was so impressed with my work that he arranged to have some very influential people look at some of my designs. They became some of my first paying clients. It was David who encouraged me to return to school."

"I still don't understand what that has to do with—"

She put a finger to his lips.

"There's more." She squeezed his hand as she unraveled the details that had changed their lives.

When she'd finished, Braxton sat back in his chair and briefly shut his eyes in pain and relief.

"So you see, she just felt that she was doing what was best for me. David could offer me the security and comfort that she had always believed I should have."

"I understand her reasons," he said, looking directly into her eyes, "but I don't understand yours. I can't see you married to Lang for any reason."

She looked away from the pressure of his eyes and the truth of his words. Did she dare tell him? If she did, there was no turning back—ever. She had to be absolutely sure of him first.

"At the time it seemed like the right thing to do. It was so important to my grandmother, and I owed her so much, Braxton. Please understand that." Her voice broke. "And I was so very lonely and hurt."

He hurried to her side and pulled his chair next to hers.

"Oh, baby." He dropped his head and pressed it

against her hand. "I'm so sorry. I didn't know." He pulled her against his chest. "I thought you didn't want me anymore." He tilted her chin up with the tip of his finger. "I guess I have quite a bit of explaining to do myself."

She sniffed back her tears and dabbed her eyes with the cotton napkin. When she looked around the room, she saw that it had filled up considerably with afternoon patrons. She wanted to be alone with him now—especially now.

"Let's go for a walk. It's getting kind of crowded." She managed a weak smile.

"That's my line," he teased. He took her hand and flashed her that irresistible, devastating smile.

"Will you two lovebirds be back?" Sophie asked with a wink. "We have some wonderful dishes prepared for dinner."

"We'll see," Tempest said, squeezing Braxton's hand and looking at him with uncertainty and a bit of hope.

"I'm sure we will," Braxton said confidently and gave Tempest's hand a tingling kiss.

They strolled slowly around the perimeter of the grounds. Tempest kept her eyes focused on the dirt road as they walked, while Braxton spoke.

"You already know that Jasmine and I knew each other from childhood. What you didn't know was that her father and my father were boyhood friends, and had always expected us to get married after we com-

169

pleted school. Her father made sure that I wasn't out of her sight by sending her to the University of Virginia."

"So you're saying that you married her because it was expected of you?" she asked incredulously. "Then what about everything you told me while we were together? You knew all along that you were going to marry her. Didn't you?" she accused.

She flung his hand away and started to storm off when he grabbed her arm and spun her around to face him.

"Are you going to listen to me or fly off the handle?" he roared. "Because if you don't listen, then we might as well end this conversation now!" His eyes burned into hers.

You're doing it again, she reminded herself. They'd never get anything settled if she continued to shut him out.

"I'm sorry," she said sheepishly.

"That's better." He smiled, obviously relieved, and released her arm. "Now can I finish?"

She nodded and he recaptured her hand as they continued their talk.

"When I returned from school, my father was in the hospital. The family never told me because they believed that it would interfere with my studies." He paused and gulped back a knot of remembrance. "Neither did they tell me that he was dying."

"I'm so sorry," she said softly and squeezed his hand.

He gave a resigned shrug and continued. "The business was going down the drain, and I had to sell the house to pay the hospital bills. By the time I wrote to you, my father was already dead. But before he died he made me promise to hold the business together. His firm meant everything to him. It wasn't until much later that I discovered that he had put everything on the line to finance my education."

"How were you supposed to hold the business together?"

"That's where Jasmine came in. Her father said that he'd refinance the company if I promised to marry his daughter."

"Didn't you tell him about us?"

"Of course I did. But it didn't matter. All he was concerned with was his daughter's happiness. Jasmine is an only child, her father's pride and joy. And if Jasmine wanted anything, her father would move heaven and earth to get it for her."

"What she wanted was you," Tempest said in a distant voice. "But what about you? Why did you cave in? Wasn't there any other way for you to get the money you needed?"

"No, there wasn't. While I was away, my father had gotten into serious debt. He owed thousands of dollars. The bank was taking steps to foreclose. If I didn't take Mr. St. Claire up on his offer, everything my father ever worked for would have been lost. Then I also found out that the reason he was in such debt was because he had put everything on the line, the entire company, to pay for my education. I couldn't let him down."

"So you had to marry Jasmine."

"Yes," he said firmly.

"Do you love her?" she asked, her heart pounding with the question.

His eyes spanned the skies, as if looking for an answer in the racing clouds. He drew a deep sigh and shook his head in regret.

"I think I did, at least in the beginning. I was so torn up and confused with everything that was going on—and then believing that you had turned your back on me was more than I could handle. I felt that I had lost everything. I needed comfort, someone I could talk with, and someone to care about me again. Jasmine provided those things."

"Even though our lives drifted apart," Tempest said in a faraway voice, finally understanding, "we were living parallel lives. Both of us were trapped in relationships for reasons other than our own."

She stopped walking and took both of his hands in her own, and stared into his eyes. "What about now? Do you love her now?" She held her breath, waiting for his response.

"No, I don't, sweetheart," he said earnestly. "Jasmine and I have been separated for two years. The night that you came to the hotel was the first time she and I have seen each other in months. I still don't understand why she showed up like that. She claims she had some time off, and she wanted to see me. But knowing Jasmine, it must have something to do with money. I filed a divorce action against her over a year ago, but she contested it."

Braxton caught the look of disappointment in her face. He pulled her into his arms.

"I promise you," he said softly, "I will be free. After this job is finished, I'll have enough capital to offer Jasmine a huge settlement. I know she'll take it this time."

"How can you be so sure?" she asked, a ray of hope lifting her voice.

"Jasmine has grown into a greedy woman, and her drinking problem doesn't help matters any," he added in obvious disgust. "She's not used to struggling for anything. And now I hear from reliable sources that she's broke. As long as I have enough money to set her straight and keep her going for a while, she'll take it."

Just then a strong gust of wind whipped through the trees, and the first drops of rain bounced off their faces. Braxton grabbed Tempest's hand and they ran toward the inn.

"Does this remind you of anything?" Braxton yelled out over the rushing wind, as they raced across the open field.

Tempest's bubbly laughter rang out across the field at the warm memory, and her heart thudded with anticipation.

Chapter Twelve

When they returned, breathless, happy, and drenched, Sophie immediately escorted them to Tempest's favorite room, scolding them all the way up the wooden stairs, against all of their halfhearted protestations.

"Naughty children," she admonished, clicking her tongue against her teeth. "You'll catch pneumonia, the both of you."

She took a huge key from the ring that hung on her rotund hip and opened the door.

"Now you two get out of those wet clothes while I start this fire. There are plenty of clean towels in the bathroom."

Braxton looked at Tempest, over Sophie's shoulder, in wide-eyed amusement.

Tempest shrugged her shoulders and grinned.

"She thinks we're married," she mouthed.

"I love the idea," he mouthed back and headed for the bathroom.

Sophie began stoking the fire while Braxton changed. Tempest took off her coat and wet shoes and began drying her hair with a towel that lay near the hearth.

When Braxton re-emerged, clad only in a towel wrapped around his narrow waist, the fire was already blazing.

Sophie clasped her plump hands together, satisfied that all was well. "I'll bring you two up a big bowl of clam chowder and a bottle of wine. How's that?" she beamed.

"Sounds perfect," Braxton said, hugging Tempest snugly around the waist, moving smoothly into the role of her husband.

"I'll be right back then." She scurried out the door and closed it with a thud.

Instantly the two burst out laughing and collapsed in a heap onto the huge four-poster canopied bed. Braxton rolled over on Tempest, his weight pinning her beneath him, all joviality removed from his voice.

"There would be nothing I'd like better than to be your husband," he whispered. His lips gently touched down on hers and currents of fire raced through her as she surrendered to his lips.

His large hands stroked her hair away from her face, trailed down her neck, and caressed her shoulders.

"Braxton," she breathed between his heady kisses.

"Hmm?"

"There's something I need to—"

His lips swept down on hers.

"I have to tell you about—" Her words were once again swallowed up in his kiss.

He kissed her long and hard, taking her breath away before he released her, sat up, and leaned on his elbow.

"So what's so urgent to interrupt a kiss like that?" he teased, placing a strand of her hair behind her ear.

"It's about my," she hesitated, "marriage."

His eyes darkened, and a bolt of fear shot straight through him. "What about it? You're not going to tell me you're in love with him, are you?"

She shook her head, got up from the bed, and crossed the room to stand in front of the fire, feeling suddenly cold with fear.

"What is it, baby? You can tell me." He went to stand behind her. "Isn't it time for the secrets and mistrust to end?" he coaxed.

She took a deep, cleansing breath. "I married David for more reasons than I told you." The butterflies flapped frantically in her stomach, making her light-headed. But she forced herself to go on. "Two months after I returned to New York, I found out—"

The slight tapping on the door interrupted her.

Braxton marched over and flung it open.

Sophie bustled past him, totally oblivious to the strained atmosphere. She placed the tray of steaming food and bottle of chilled wine on the small table by the window.

"Eat up now, before it gets cold," she ordered. "If you need anything, just pull that rope over there." She pointed to a tasseled rope that hung by the bedpost. She ambled back toward the door, then stopped midway. "Where's my head?" she mumbled, tapping her forehead with the palm of her hand. "This is for you."

She took a long, pink terry-cloth robe off her arm and handed it to Tempest. "It was a birthday present about five years ago. Never worn. You're welcome to it." She pressed it into Tempest's hand.

"Thank you, Sophie." Tempest bent down and kissed her cheek. "You didn't have to."

"You're one of my favorite customers. It's my pleasure. Now sit down and eat. I just hope you bring your handsome husband back again. It's about time we had a chance to see him." With that she was out of the room and gone.

With that distraction aside, Braxton turned to face Tempest, his mind racing with crazy possibilities of what she planned to tell him. What else could have been so earth shattering to contribute to her marrying David Lang?

A slight tremor raced through her at the look he shot her way. What must he be thinking? She massaged her temples. He'd never forgive her—not for this. She was sure of it. But she had to tell him.

She nearly jumped out of her skin when his deep voice filled the room.

"Are you going to finish telling me, or are you going to make me guess?"

She looked up into his eyes, and the look of love and concern that radiated from them gave her the assurance she needed.

"I was pregnant, Braxton," she said finally.

He felt as if a train had rammed him in his stomach. So that was it! She married Lang because she'd gotten pregnant by him. He sank down on the bed. So maybe Lang wasn't such a bad guy after all. He did the honorable thing and married her. He shook his head in disbelief, then anger and a sense of ultimate betrayal suddenly replaced his astonishment.

"You didn't wait very long after me before you jumped in bed with someone else and then got pregnant no less," he spat out.

She was like a blur before his eyes. The slap across his face came so hard and fast, it twisted his head.

"How dare you?" she hissed, her breathing coming in rapid bursts. "Do you think so little of me that you'd believe something like that? And I thought you'd understand." She hurled the words at him. "But you're not capable of it."

He jumped up from the bed and in two quick strides stood in front of her. "What do you expect me to think?" he growled, his eyes blazing like burning coals. He grabbed her shoulders and shook her. "Tell me! What do you expect me to think?"

"I expect you to know that...that baby—" Her voice broke as tears began to flow. "My daughter couldn't be anyone else's but yours!"

"What?" He couldn't believe what he was hearing. "You mean—you were—but you—why didn't you— Oh, God!" He sank back down on the bed and pulled her down beside him. Now what she had said that night in the car came back to him at full force. She had slipped and said *our* daughter. Now it all made sense.

"Oh, baby, I'm so sorry." He hugged her with all of his strength. "It was just that all of a sudden I got so hurt and angry, I just couldn't see straight. Please forgive me," he begged, showering her with tender kisses.

"I would," she gasped, "if I could only breathe."

He started to chuckle, realizing that he was crushing her in his hold, and he loosened his grip. "These shoes are kind of tight when they're on the other foot. I guess you must be rubbing off on me. It's usually you who jumps to conclusions."

"I'm sorry I slapped you," she said, rubbing his cheek.

"I more than deserved it," he smiled. His eyes met and searched hers. Several moments passed before he could speak. "Tell me everything about her," he said in wonderment, "starting with her name."

Tempest was elated beyond belief and she enthusiastically spun out stories about her favorite subject—Kai.

When she'd stopped for breath, they both smiled at each other for countless moments, assessing each other in a totally new light.

Braxton felt a barrage of new emotions he couldn't quite understand. He felt powerful yet humbled by his newfound fatherhood. He felt frightened at the prospect—and angry that so many years had been taken away from him. What bothered him most was that there was a little girl out there who was his, and he didn't even know what she looked like—and the woman that he loved beyond reason was the wife of the next congressman from New York.

As Tempest watched the montage of emotions flicker across his eyes, she felt a sensation of relief that she'd never imagined possible. It was finally over and he didn't hate her as she had so feared. However, with the sense of relief was also a deep feeling of regret.

She had participated in depriving this loving man of being a part of his daughter's life for so long. And he would make such a wonderful father. Then a harsher reality set in. Maybe she should have never told him at all. That way he could never miss what he knew nothing about. Now she'd opened up a new door, but it was barred to him, and it would stay closed. David would make sure that it did. How could she now take away what she had so recently given? She had to now tell him what David had threatened to do. He deserved to know that as well. Then maybe somehow, some way, they could work it out together.

"Braxton," she said softly, easing into his thoughts. "There's more—"

Braxton leaned against the window frame, staring blankly out at the pouring rain, wishing that somehow the waters could magically wash them away to a place where they could all be together and away from the clutches of David Lang. There had to be a way to fight him without losing everything in the process. He wouldn't lose Tempest again, and now he had the added motivation of his daughter to consider.

Tempest stepped up quietly behind him, hugging him around his waist and pressing her head against his bare back.

"What are we going to do?" she asked softly.

He ran his hand across his beard and sighed deeply. "For now we'll just have to wait and see what happens after the election in the fall, as you said," he told her slowly. "By that time my divorce should be final."

"But what if he wins? I could—"

"We'll cross that bridge when we come to it." He slipped an arm around her waist and eased her snugly against him. "One thing's for sure," he drawled, "I'm never going to let you go again. Don't let that thought ever enter your beautiful head. I'll do whatever I have to do."

He leaned down and pressed his lips to her opened mouth. She reached up on tiptoe and stretched her arms around his neck, pulling him closer.

He spread his fingers across the expanse of her back and caressed her spine, sending shivers of delight pulsing through her veins. She let out a low moan of pleasure when he pressed the length of his rock-hard body solidly against hers, the thin fabric of the towel giving evidence of his rising ardor.

His hot lips trailed fiery kisses across her cheeks, her lips, then down her long neck. Taking one hand, he slid it under her sweater and masterfully released the clasp of her bra. With sure fingers he cupped her left breast in his hand, kneading the ripe nipple between his fingers.

He heard her quick intake of breath at his ministrations—and in one sweeping motion lifted her up into his arms and carried her to the canopied bed.

With slow deliberation, he undressed her piece by piece. She lay perfectly still, relishing the look of intense desire that shot through his ebony eyes. Easing himself down next to her, he began at the top of her head, his satiny lips and knowing hands meticulously arousing every inch of her body.

Involuntarily she began to move in slow sensuous motion beneath his fingertips. Her slender hands reached for him, but he gently stretched her arms above her head and held them there while he placed his body solidly atop hers, rendering her incapable of movement.

"Not yet," he groaned in her ear, his hot breath vibrating down to her toes. "I want to take my time with you."

His free hand glided over her shimmering body, teasing, taunting and caressing, while skillfully threading his web of inescapable yearning within her.

"Braxton," she whispered. "I love you so much. I—" Her words were swallowed up in his kiss. His smooth tongue danced with hers in a ritual as old as time itself.

He held her fiercely against him, absorbing her very being through his pores, afraid that if he should dare to let go, this miracle that he had found would slip away like so many particles of sand through his fingers. How could he be so blessed as to have a second chance with the woman of his dreams? He wanted to shout out to the world his joy and his frustration—that what he held in his arms was still just out of his reach.

As she lay captive in his hold, savoring the pleasure that he had aroused within her, she looked into his exquisite face, and she truly understood the magnificence of true love. She knew that with this man, they could overcome anything together. For so many years she'd lain awake at night longing for his touch, the sound of his voice, the sparkle in his eyes. She couldn't lose him again, she knew at last, as she smothered his lips with her own.

With nimble fingers he loosened the knot that held the towel around his waist and effortlessly tossed it to the floor. He let out a soft moan as hard flesh met supple flesh, heartbeat meeting heartbeat in perfect rhythm.

He stroked her with tender, pleasure-seeking fingers, awakening sensations in an all new, unbelievable way. The smooth tips of his fingers inched over her body, preparing a pathway for his eager mouth. As his lips touched down on her inflamed body, currents of erotic desire jettisoned to her center. A cry of total surrender escaped her lips as she lay shuddering beneath him, wanting to enfold him within her. But still he held her immobile while he tantalized her with feather-soft kisses and stroked the hollow of her neck with his scintillating tongue.

"I'll always love you, always," he whispered in her ear, separating her thighs with a well-placed knee.

She moved her hips seductively beneath him, enticing him with her obvious need of him, sure that she was no longer able to be denied.

But his control was impeccable. Though the doorway was opened and waiting for him to cross the threshold, he would not. Instead he tortured her with sultry words of love, masterful hands, and irresistible lips, prolonging the moment to the fullest.

But her impatience grew to unmanageable proportions, and she thrust her hips firmly against him, uniting them in the tempo that bound them perfectly to each other. Her body seemed to vibrate with liquid fire as bursts of desire shook her. His hardness electrified her, and she couldn't disguise her body's pulsating response to his penetrating movements.

He cried out at the incendiary sensation that rocketed through him and sank helplessly into the smoldering folds of her yielding body. He ground his hips against hers as her nails mercilessly raked his back, making him throw his head back in pain and pleasure. His large hands reached beneath her and pulled her tightly against him, while she wrapped her long shapely legs around his broad back and gave herself up to the intangible delight of his throbbing undulations.

As they moved together over the hills and valleys of their private world, Tempest was filled with a sense of inner peace and infinite completeness. He filled her, not only in body, but in spirit. She knew that he gave all of himself to her, as he tenderly administered to all of her secret places.

This time between them was different from any other, Braxton thought, as he moved lovingly over her. No longer were they bent on quenching a purely physical need but instead met each other on a higher plane. This was more than a release of passion, he thought, as his body continued to drive them forward. This was the most precious gift a man and woman could give to each other—total surrender of their being. Tears of pure bliss clouded his eyes as he held her to him, wanting this time to never end.

As they climbed higher to the mountaintop of fulfillment, all of nature seemed to rejoice in their union. The pounding rain beat mercilessly against the window pane and the heavens ignited with bolts of brilliant light. The world seemed to spin crazily on its axis while the birds fluttered madly through the trees crying out in perfect synchronism with the melting of body and spirit.

Then the sun magically burst forth through the storm clouds bathing the lovers in its nourishing light, drying up the rain, and seemingly blessing them in its rays.

They gave themselves up to the ceaseless pleasure they had ignited within each other. Together they merged with the heavens, and earth became a distant place as they soared over the boundaries that held them captive, to eclipse in a single moment of blinding, uninhibited release.

When she awoke, the sun was beginning to set, illuminating the horizon in blazing orange light. She turned on her side and tenderly stroked the perfect face that lay next to her. No longer was she afraid or ashamed of what she had done, because she knew deep in her heart that they were meant to be.

Slowly Braxton's eyes fluttered open, and he bathed her in the warmth of his smile. "Hello, stormy one," he breathed and cradled her in his arms.

She returned his smile with a tender kiss and gently eased herself from his hold. "I've got to get back to the city," she said hesitantly. "The primary is tonight, and David will be expecting me."

He sat up in bed. "Do you have to go?"

She couldn't meet his piercing gaze. "I don't have much of a choice. It would look pretty strange if I didn't."

Braxton lay back down and stared up at the flowered canopy. "If you have to, then I guess you should," he said, the disappointment apparent in his voice.

"Please don't sound like that," she pleaded. "I don't want to leave but—"

"Then stay!" He swung his long legs over the side of the bed and stood up beside her, pulling her into his arms. "I need you," he whispered in her ear.

"I need you, too, but I have to go back." He released her and turned away. "Then you'd better get dressed," he said in a toneless voice.

"Aren't you coming?"

"No. I think I'll stay here tonight, and go back in the morning. With my luck I'd go back tonight and Jasmine wouldn't have moved out yet. I couldn't handle that, too."

✕

She stood facing him in the doorway, once again with a heavy heart.

"When will I see you again?" he asked.

"I'm not sure."

"Try to make it soon. I don't know how long I can wait." He gave her a lopsided smile.

"Everything is going to work out"—her voice broke—"isn't it?"

He wrapped her in his arms and gently rocked her. "It has to, sweetheart." He kissed the top of her head. "It just has to."

She stepped back and took a deep breath, then reached into her purse for her wallet. Flipping through the inserts, she found what she was looking for.

"Here." She handed him a tiny picture. "This is our daughter."

He looked at the cherubic face with eyes so much like his own and found himself lacking words. His heart pumped wildly in his chest, and his throat constricted with a knot of joy. A single tear fell from his eyes and dotted the little face before him. When he looked up, Tempest was gone.

Chapter Thirteen

When Tempest and Kai arrived at David's campaign headquarters in lower Manhattan, the huge room radiated from the energetic euphoria which had swept up everyone there. In less than an hour, the polling sites would be closed, and the votes would be in. From all indications David was way ahead of his Republican opponent.

Hundreds of diehard followers raced from phone to phone, pulled information from computer printouts, and yelled out updates and words of encouragement across the room. The noise level was deafening.

"Who are all these people?" Kai shouted over the bedlam.

"Daddy's friends," Tempest yelled back. She held tightly on to Kai's hand, as they inched their way over the mounds of paper and discarded coffee cups.

"Where's Mr. Lang?" Tempest asked one harried worker who had a phone in each hand.

The redheaded woman pointed in the direction of a closed door on the far side of the office.

Tempest let out a deep sigh of relief when she entered the cool and tranquil quarters that David had secured for himself. She really was not up to the noise and confusion that this night held—and certainly not after her interlude with Braxton. But she couldn't dwell on that now.

When they entered, David gave them an engaging smile, motioning them to have a seat while he completed his phone conversation. Kai instead ran over to him and plopped down on his lap.

Tempest felt a sick sensation rock her stomach as she took a seat on the long, overstuffed couch and viewed the exchange between Kai and David.

She adores him, Tempest thought miserably. How could she ever take that away from her by telling Kai about her real father? Kai had always been such a sensitive child and had suffered silently through the tension that existed between her and David. Fortunately Kai didn't know the real David and how vindictive he could be. Her own newfound discovery of the dark side of his personality still had her reeling. How was this ever going to work out, she worried. David was a powerful man, with or without a congressional seat. Maybe it would be best if they just left everything the way it had been. But she knew that now, it could never be the same ever again.

"I hope you're not going to have that look on your face when they announce the primary results," David said, cutting into her disturbing thoughts.

"Oh, I'm sorry," she mumbled with a half-smile. "I was just thinking about something at the office."

He walked over to where she stood, holding Kai's hand, while Kai looked up adoringly at him. He placed a perfunctory kiss on Tempest's cheek.

"You look very lovely this evening," he said, admiring her black dress and gold accessories.

"What about me, Daddy?" Kai cried, pulling on his navy blue jacket.

He reached down and picked her up, giving her a big hug. "You look beautiful, my darling girl. Daddy's girl always looks beautiful," he said over Kai's shoulder, giving Tempest a self-satisfied smile.

Tempest felt her stomach pitch. He was going to make this as difficult as possible for her. He seemed to take a macabre pleasure in seeing her squirm. What had happened to him?

"Can I get you two anything, or have you already had dinner?"

"Nothing for me, thanks," Tempest said.

"I'm starved!" declared Kai.

David gave a light chuckle. "The story of your life," he teased. "I'll have something sent in." He made a quick call to the front desk and ordered a platter of assorted sandwiches, a quart of milk, and a carafe of coffee.

While Kai sat contentedly eating her fare, Tempest and David sat in front of the big-screen television, watching the election results. According to the latest polls, David continued to maintain a steady lead. His victory seemed imminent.

The phones in the front office, as well as in David's, were ringing off the hook with calls from workers in the field sending up-to-the-minute information and messages of congratulations. A concession speech by his opponent was only moments away.

By nine o'clock, with all of the major districts tallied across the state, David was declared the indisputable winner. The shouts of victory reverberated throughout the office. News reporters and television cameras were positioned outside the campaign headquarters, waiting for the victor to appear. David bided his time, soaking in the adoration and words of support from his massive team of workers.

This is the moment that I've worked so hard for. He moved confidently through the crowd of revelers, shaking hands and receiving numerous wet kisses on his cheeks. A momentary pang of guilt ran through him when he saw Tempest's face across the crowded room. He nearly destroyed her in order to achieve his ends, and sometimes he wasn't sure if it was worth it. But then when he reminded himself of the power that was just within reach, his doubts about his morals quickly dissipated.

His closest aide, Ray Turner, pushed his way through the throng and whispered in his ear. "The press is getting pretty impatient out there, David. I don't think you should keep them waiting any longer."

"You're right. Let them know I'll be right out."

"Sure thing."

David motioned to Tempest to join him at the front door so that they could face the cameras and innumerable questions together.

❧

"Mr. Lang, what tactics are you going to use against your opponent in the fall?"

"My opponent is very weak on the issues of housing and balancing budgets. As you know, my firm has undertaken the redevelopment of a block of land in New Jersey. That apartment complex is to be reserved exclusively for low income and homeless families."

"But, Mr. Lang, how is that helping your constituency here in New York?"

"Once that project is off the ground by the summer, and successful, as I know that it will be," he said smiling expansively to the crowd, "I intend to replicate it throughout New York State."

"We understand, Mr. Lang, that your wife is in charge of the design. Is that true?"

David put his arm around Tempest's shoulder. "She certainly is." He placed a light kiss on her cheek.

"I am a firm believer in family and families sticking together. After all, the family is the foundation on which this country was built."

"Do you intend to let your wife's firm work on the New York project as well?"

David gave a wry chuckle. "If I did that, it would certainly be a conflict of interest. However, my wife will be working in a voluntary consultant capacity."

"How do you feel, Mrs. Lang, about your husband's victory tonight?"

"I'm very proud of him," Tempest said softly. "He worked very hard for this night, and I'm sure that if he sets his mind to it, he can accomplish anything."

David immediately felt the undercurrent of her well-chosen words and diplomatically ended any further discussions.

"It's getting pretty late, ladies and gentlemen, and it's well past my daughter's bedtime." He lifted Kai up into his arms, and she snuggled against his shoulder, rubbing her eyes. The effect was perfect, as the crowd of cameramen and reporters avidly documented the touching scene.

"One last question, Mr. Lang," came a voice from the back of the crowd. "Where exactly is the housing complex that is currently under way and what was it before development?"

"The site is located in Bloomfield, New Jersey. It was previously a manufacturing warehouse. All of you are welcome to come out for a tour any time."

The unidentified man jotted down the information and then hurried away.

David felt a strange sense of foreboding as he waved good night, but quickly shook it off as he ushered Tempest back inside the headquarters.

"Nice touch," he whispered maliciously into her ear. "Don't cross me, Tempest. You'll regret it. I've come too far for any interference."

She discreetly shrugged his hand off her shoulder.

"I have no idea what you're talking about," she said through clenched teeth. "You've made yourself perfectly clear."

She strode across the room and retrieved her coat and Kai's. David followed closely behind her and closed the door, Kai fully asleep in his arms. She spun to face him, her face a mask of rage and disgust.

"You've gotten what you wanted, David. Everything except me. You'll never have me, not ever again. I don't know what it's going to take to get away from you, David," she said with newfound conviction. "But whatever it is, I'll find the way."

With that she snatched Kai from his arms and stormed out the door.

✖

It had been over five hours since Ella had been

taken into surgery. Tempest nervously paced the floor of the hospital waiting room, jumping at the sound of every closing door.

"Honey, why don't you sit down?" Clara pleaded. "You won't do Ella any good if you exhaust yourself."

"The doctors said it shouldn't take more than three hours," Tempest cried, twisting her hands as she spoke. "Something must have gone wrong. I just know it!" She raked a trembling hand through her hair.

"Come over here and sit down," Clara coaxed. She helped Tempest toward a leather recliner. "I'm going over to the cafeteria and get some coffee. Do you want anything?"

"Some coffee would be fine," she mumbled.

"Everything's gonna be just fine," Clara said softly, patting Tempest's shoulder.

Tempest sat there for several minutes, staring blankly into space, oblivious to the nonstop traffic of doctors, nurses, and patients crossing in front of the glass-enclosed waiting room.

So much had happened in such a short space of time. Her thoughts and feelings were so jumbled and twisted she didn't know what to do or how to feel. Her entire well-planned life was turned upside down. All the truths that she had built her world on were lies, crumbling under her feet. The very people that she had held above all others had disappointed and betrayed her. When was she ever going to take control of her own life, and stop relinquishing her free will to satisfy others?

She got up from the chair and once again resumed her pacing, when Braxton entered the waiting room.

"Hi," he said gently. "I thought you could use some company."

Her heart lifted and lodged in her throat at the sight of him. She felt the warmth of his smiling eyes melt away the ice that had formed around her heart. She flung herself into his arms, pressing her head against his chest, fighting desperately to control the tears which threatened to overflow.

"How did you know?" she sniffed, sinking deeper into his comforting embrace.

"I called your office this morning. Bridgette told me you were here." He hugged her tighter, wishing that he could absorb her hurt. "Have you heard anything yet?"

"No," she said in a weak voice. "It's been hours."

"I'm sure that if there was anything to report, one way or the other, sweetheart, you would have heard something. We'll just have to be patient."

We, how wonderful that sounds. She wiped her eyes and gently eased out of his hold, the ramifications of his visit suddenly hitting home. What if, by chance, David should show up? How would she ever explain Braxton's presence?

"Listen," she said, placing both of her hands on

his chest and looking up imploringly into his eyes. "I really appreciate your being here. But—"

"I know. Don't say it. I just wanted to lend you some moral support."

"Thank you," she said softly. "It just makes me love you all the more."

"Call me...when you can."

"I will."

He gave her a quick kiss on the cheek and was gone.

Tempest returned to her seat and continued her silent vigil, when simultaneously Clara and Dr. James entered the room. She slowly rose and tried to read his eyes, but they remained impassive. He pulled his surgical cap from his head and wiped his brow with the back of his hand. Clara hurried to Tempest's side and together they faced the doctor.

He took a deep breath before he spoke. "It took a lot longer than expected, but I have to hand it to your husband, Mrs. Lang. He certainly got the best surgeons."

Tempest held her breath.

"We can't be positive," he continued, "because she's not out of danger yet. However, everything looks good. The operation went extremely well. She's a tough lady." He finally gave into a smile, and Tempest let out an audible sigh of relief.

"Thank God," Clara whispered, hugging a trembling Tempest to her.

"Can we see her?" Tempest asked, her voice about to break.

"She'll be in recovery for several hours. You might as well go home. But I'm sure that the surgeon will want to speak with you before you leave. I just wanted to be the bearer of good news," he added with a tender smile.

Tempest extended her hand to Dr. James. "Thank you, doctor—for everything."

"Just doing my job." He gave her an encouraging smile. "Take care of yourself." He turned and strode down the corridor, wondering briefly what it would be like to be loved by a woman like her.

✂

Weeks after his primary victory, David should have been jubilant. Instead he stood staring out onto the street below his office window. His smooth brow was knitted in a deep frown. His thick brown eyebrows formed one straight line.

Why were the EPA investigators at the site? They'd received the reports and had been out there at least a half dozen times already. Why this sudden resurgence of interest months into the project? There had to be a reason.

He'd been trying to contact Joe Ackerman for days, but he seemed to have vanished. That mildly concerned him. What concerned him more was that now the EPA had taken their own soil samples. Specialists had been sent out to test the land, and the results would be in any day now.

Hopefully they wouldn't find what he feared, if Joe's experiment had worked as he claimed that it would. He had been systematically treating the soil with a nontraceable chemical with the intention of obliterating any traces of toxins. But if the investigators found anything—anything at all—there was sure to be an investigation, and he would be ruined.

Then there was the Thorne woman to contend with. She hadn't held up her end of the bargain as far as he was concerned. If she had, Tempest would have never asked for a divorce. He was sure of it. Her job was to be so visible that Thorne and Tempest would never have an opportunity to be together. She'd failed miserably, according to his sources. Yet she'd been calling his office like clockwork, demanding the other half of her money. He'd have to find a way to deal with that albatross. He shook his head in frustration and jammed his hands into his pants pockets.

Everything seemed to be rushing to a head. Either it would all burst wide open or slowly dissolve. He only wished he knew which it would be.

᙭

It was just after three o'clock, and Jasmine was on her fourth martini. She sat alone in a back booth of

Houlihan's Bar and Grill on Thirty-fourth Street, wallowing in her dilemma.

She was due back in Atlanta in less than a week for inventory, and she had yet to secure all of the money she needed to buy back the merchandise she had pawned. Fortunately no one had discovered the duplicates that she had replaced the missing pieces with. She had her years of study in art and sculpting to thank for that. But she was sure that her replacements would never hold up under the close scrutiny of the assessors.

Damn that David Lang, she fumed, finishing off her drink. She'd done what he'd asked, hadn't she? She motioned to the bartender for a refill. Wasn't she at the site as often as she could be? After all, didn't a woman deserve some relaxation and entertainment since her husband refused to have anything to do with her? Which brought her fuzzy thoughts to Tempest.

Who did she think she was anyway? She thought she'd be rid of her once and for all when she returned to New York. But she turned up just like a bad penny. She gulped down her drink and slapped two twenty dollar bills on the table. She had a few choice words for that hussy before it was all over. But she'd have to deal with David first.

She stumbled over to the bar and crooked her finger at the bartender. "Thanks for such *great* service 'weetie," she slurred.

"Do you have someone to take you home, miss?"

"Oh, I sure wish you could, cutie," she mumbled, leaning forward on the countertop with both elbows. "But I have bizness to take care of. I'm gonna fix them good."

Her bloodshot eyes rolled in her head. She snatched up her purse with as much dignity as she could summon and gravitated toward the revolving door.

The bartender shook his head and wiped down the counter with a damp cloth.

Jasmine managed to get behind the wheel of her lemon yellow Mustang convertible and gently edged out into the early afternoon traffic.

She'd go to David first and demand her money. If he refused, then she'd just have to threaten him with the information she'd overheard at the restaurant. But what if he didn't buy it, she thought, narrowly missing a car on her left. She swerved to her right and got back in her lane, her heart pounding at the close call.

The near miss momentarily cleared her head as she skidded to a halt at the red light. She took a deep breath and when the light turned green she turned onto Madison Avenue and headed uptown to David's office. She shook her head to clear it, and took a quick peek in her rearview mirror and decided to put on her dark glasses.

With a shaky hand she reached into the glove compartment for her glasses and slipped them over her glassy eyes. She had to keep herself together, she reminded herself. Too much depended on her pulling this off.

David jumped at the ringing of his personal phone. He'd been waiting hours for some news from the site. This had to be the call.

"Yes, Annie," he barked into the mouthpiece.

"Uh, Mr. Lang, there are some gentlemen here to see you."

David felt the pulse in his temple begin to throb. "Who are they?"

They say they're from the EPA and there's a Detective Lloyd with them, sir," she whispered.

"Give me a few minutes and then send them in."

"Yes, Mr. Lang."

David felt his heart race, and for the first time he felt stark fear and vulnerability. He crossed the room and sat down behind his desk. Slight beads of perspiration dotted his forehead and trickled down his back. He had to pull himself together. Maybe there was still a way out of this. He just needed time to think. But there wasn't time. He should call his lawyer, he thought, his mind racing in all directions. Yes, that's what he would do.

But before he could reach for the phone, the door swung open and three men dressed in cheap business suits entered his office.

"I told them to wait," Annie whined, her voice bordering on hysteria.

"It's all right, Annie," David said, trying to compose his thoughts. "Come in, gentlemen. What can I do for you?" He stood to greet them.

"Mr. Lang, I'm Detective Lloyd and these gentlemen are from the EPA. I have a search warrant for your office." He tossed the warrant on David's desk.

"A search warrant! What on earth for?" Why hadn't he removed the original report from the file as he had started to do? David felt his entire future slowly toppling into rubble.

"We've already seized Mr. Ackerman's files, Mr. Lang," the detective stated flatly, as his narrow eyes roamed the exquisite office in obvious envy.

David's insides turned over and formed a rock-hard knot in the pit of his stomach. What could they have found? Probably everything. *That idiot!*

He's a cool one, the detective thought, as he watched David review the search warrant.

The two investigators proceeded to go through every file, every record and business transaction related to the complex.

"I think we have what we're looking for," said the smaller of the two investigators. He held up a manila folder marked CONFIDENTIAL.

The detective turned to David, a look of satisfaction sparkling in his eyes. "Mr. Lang, you have the right to remain silent—"

The monotone voice droned on, spewing out the Miranda rights. David felt his knees go weak, but he refused to let them see him break.

"I'd like to make a phone call, if you don't mind, Detective," David said in a firm voice.

"You can get your one phone call down at the station, Mr. Lang," Lloyd stated as he placed David's hands behind his back and locked the handcuffs with a sound of finality.

David held his head high, looking at no one or anything, as he was escorted out of his office and down the long corridor to the bank of elevators.

As he passed his astonished staff who stood by in stunned silence, a flash of light went off in his eyes. When his vision cleared, a moment of instant recollection and the stark reality of his situation became transparent. Behind the lens of the camera was the same man from the back of the crowd on the night of the primary. David would have laughed if it wasn't so ironic, realizing that a lowly reporter was the seed behind his downfall. What a person wouldn't do for a byline, he thought morosely.

"*Touché*," he said softly, as he passed the reporter and continued toward the elevator.

Just as they reached the elevator door, Jasmine staggered off ready to charge into David's office. The cloudy vision in front of her stopped her in her tracks. She stepped aside to let the group pass, swaying unsteadily against the wall, disbelief masking her face.

"I guess our business is concluded, Mrs. Thorne," David said matter-of-factly and stepped through the doors.

Jasmine's mind reeled. David arrested? Someone obviously had the same information she had. Only they were lucky enough to get to him first. What was she going to do? She knew she could never survive a jail term. She just couldn't. Panic gripped her like a vise. Her breath came in short rapid bursts, and she was sure that she would faint. She felt herself slowly sinking to the floor, but with her last ounce of reserve she pressed the down button and stumbled into the elevator.

Her head spun and she burst through the revolving doors and headed in the direction of her car. Blindly she fumbled through her purse for her car keys and slid behind the wheel. She had to get away where no one could find her. That's what she'd do. She'd go somewhere, change her name and start over.

She darted out into traffic, her car weaving in and out of the racing automobiles. But where would she go, she thought, hysteria gripping her. She didn't have any money. She'd just drive and drive, she thought, through the haze of her consciousness.

×≈×

He didn't see the car that sped out from behind the parked van until it was too late. The driver of the eighteen-wheeler tried in vain to veer away from the speeding yellow automobile, and forever the look of peace in the driver's eyes would haunt him. In that final instant, when Jasmine's eyes met death head on, and twisted metal ripped through supple flesh, she thought: *At last I am free.*

Chapter Fourteen

The entire investigation and David's resulting trial took several months. He'd been fined two million dollars and would serve a minimum of three years in prison. After numerous court appearances and presentation of contracts and supporting statements, Braxton and Tempest were cleared of any culpability.

After Jasmine's funeral and the completion of the trial, Braxton returned to Virginia to try to get his life back in order. Yet even though he was free, he didn't want his freedom this way. Too many people and too many lives had been hurt in the process.

As he wandered out into the yard of his Virginia home, he wondered how he could have done things differently. He'd been so sure that he would have gotten Tempest back, and his daughter. Now that, too, seemed only a fantasy in view of the past few months.

Tempest was still tied to New York, trying to unravel the legal maze that David had constructed around his multitude of enterprises. There didn't seem to be any chance of her divorce coming through any-time soon, and Kai still didn't know that he was her father.

He'd called Tempest consistently at first, but she was always in a somber and distant mood, until his calls became fewer and farther between. Then he just stopped. If it wasn't for Scott, who stuck by him every minute, he didn't know what he would have done throughout those lonely and terrifying days.

The summer sun beat down unmercifully on his bare back, but he took no notice. He sat down, forlorn-ly in the garden, thinking about his life and the long empty days that lay ahead, when the presence of some-one behind him cast a long shadow over his shoulder. He turned, lifting his hand to shield his eyes from the glaring sun. His heart lifted in exhilaration and dis-belief.

"Tempest?" he said warily, slowly rising from the grassy ground.

The figure moved slowly forward as if in a dream. He stepped cautiously toward what must surely be an apparition, not daring to hope that she could be real. The sun cleared from in front of his eyes and cast a brilliant halo around the figure before him. He could-n't stop his heart from racing, and before he realized what he was doing, he had grabbed her in his arms, crushing her slender frame against him, having to be sure that she was real.

She, too, clung to him. Her own joy at the feel of him sent her spirits soaring over the clouds.

His hungry mouth swept down on hers, drowning in the sweet sensation of her lips.

"Tempest, baby," he breathed. "How...why?" He held on to her, afraid to let go.

"It's over," she whispered breathlessly. "It's over."

He instantly stepped back and held her at arm's length, desperately searching her eyes, not daring to hope. But the radiance of her smile released the last of his doubts.

"My divorce papers came through yesterday. It's final," she said slowly.

"What? You didn't tell me—"

"I know. I was just so afraid that something would go wrong at the last minute, or that David would change his mind. I had to be sure."

He took her hand and pulled her down on the grass beside him. He caressed her face with his eyes. "You've been so distant over the months. I thought you'd given up on us and didn't want to tell me."

"Never," she said, shaking her head, and taking his face in her hands. "Never again will I give up on us. That is, of course, if you still want me."

"Want you?" He pulled her into his arms. "How could I ever stop wanting you?"

Braxton slowly released her and sat back on his haunches, his brow wrinkling in curiosity. "What made David agree to the divorce?"

"He's changed, Braxton," she said in a faraway voice. "I think that all of this mess has made him realize that you can't use people the way that he did—and that money is not the answer. We had a long talk. He told me everything, including how he paid Jasmine to come to New York to keep a wedge between us and how he blackmailed her into doing it. He even told me how he paid off my clients to drop their accounts with my firm.

"But even after all of that, I still feel sorry for him. He let his blind ambition destroy everything in his path, and now all that he worked for is gone."

She looked off into the horizon, her profile cutting a sharp image against the flowery backdrop.

Braxton uttered a deep sigh and silently wished that things could have turned out differently for Jasmine as well.

Tempest instinctively felt his remorse and reached out to gently touch his hand.

"It wasn't your fault," she said, her voice full of tender understanding.

"I know that rationally, but emotionally I can't help but feel that I could have done things differently—helped her, changed her somehow. I still can't believe that she'd done what the police in Atlanta said she did."

"There's no way to change the past," she said

softly, her eyes full of a newfound wisdom. "But we do have it within our power to mold our future by learning from our mistakes."

"We made a lot of them, you and I."

She smiled and nodded. "And we'll probably make more in the future. But we'll make them together—and not let other people change what we know in our hearts to be right."

Braxton nodded in silent agreement, feeling a sense of relief that he hadn't felt in ages. Then a frightening realization struck him. His short-lived spark of hope was quickly extinguished. What about Kai? What if she refused to accept him into her life? He couldn't bear that, not after what he and Tempest had endured.

"But what about—"

They both looked up toward the house. Clara walked slowly around the perimeter of the house and approached the sitting couple, with Kai in tow.

Braxton sat frozen. His dark eyes darted to Tempest, apprehension and a very real fear lighting the ebony pools.

She knows, Tempest said with her eyes, her own heart racing as she rose. She silently prayed that their first meeting would work out. She didn't know what she would do if it didn't.

Clara stood back and coaxed Kai forward. Timidly she approached, her tiny hands folded in front of her, her eyes glued to the green grass.

After what seemed an eternity, she stood before

his crouched body, nervously digging the toe of her leather shoes in the dirt.

She was more beautiful than any picture could capture, he thought, his chest constricting in a knot of fatherly pride, as he silently looked on his daughter, afraid to move. What could he possibly say to her? How could he ever make things right between them?

Then ever so slowly, her long lashes lifted, and her sparkling dark eyes rested on his face. For several moments they viewed each other in silence, while Braxton's mind raced with each passing second, searching for the right words to say.

And as if his prayers were answered cautiously, the beginnings of a smile tipped the corners of her lips. She took one hesitant step forward and then another, until she was practically in his lap. Then in a style all her own, she asked in a squeaky voice, "Well, Daddy, are you just going to sit there, or give me a kiss?"

Braxton's heart sang out in jubilation, all of his doubts and fears swept away with the summer breeze, his own smile of elation more dazzling than the sun. He stretched out his arms to his daughter, and she eagerly entered his embrace, burying her face in the hollow of his neck.

As he held her body tenderly next to his, he looked up into the misty eyes of Tempest. They smiled and knew that finally the future was theirs—to have and to hold—forever!